When the Bough Breaks

Tom West

authorHOUSE®

AuthorHouse™ UK
1663 Liberty Drive
Bloomington, IN 47403 USA
www.authorhouse.co.uk
Phone: 0800.197.4150

Published by AuthorHouse 01/06/2016

ISBN: 978-1-5049-9711-9 (sc)
ISBN: 978-1-5049-9712-6 (e)

Back page information website links

(1) **http://www.upgrademylock.com/home-security/ threats/**

(2) https://www.youtube.com/watch?v=PhPJmEt8cmI

I would like to take this opportunity to thank everybody in the Ring o Bells pub as I asked the customers of this problem what sort of stories they would like?

I listened to their individual requests and did my best to come up with this story that covers, crime, sex and murder and also the mysterious of the John-Do's body found on the M54 that was recently reported in the local newspapers….. God bless his soul

I would like to thank Des, the Landlord of The Ring O Bells pub and his wife Kelly; they keep a very entertaining and friendly pub. We have had celebrities from all over the world come in and visit this pub on a regular basis.

Friends who have inspired contents and growth of the novel I would like to say a big thank you to them too.

Charlie, Nicky, Steve, Emma, Dawn, Donna, Ian, Jo, and many more. The local window cleaner Gary. The charity run fruit and veg shop in high Street giving the best deals the charity shop on the high Street and across the road the old Post Office coffee shop.

So a great big thank you to you all and even the names that I have not mentioned in the book.

Mario Lemieux thank you for the bottle of wine Mario it was superb.

A big thanks you to Lesley Ann Fozzard who is a true spiritualist for the celebrities' Spiritual house cleansing for new homes and old.

Heaven Skincare Sinful
Hugs and kisses Tattnall

A big thank you to Keith Cox who fixed my Apple Mac. Computer company name, apple.me.uk telephone number (01952) 898011.
Bengal Spice 15 Burton Street Dawley, Telford, Shropshire.

MOT's are US Stafford Park 4

TMC Telford Motorcycle Centre Stafford Park 4

Crystals Cupcakes – (my favourite coffee shop)
Telephone number (01952) 324215

What Sits and Doodahs house clearances and antique shop
079 0202 7910/(07870) 845569
Nigel Thoma and Lisa Barden

Tan Me Style Me (01952) 357577
The finest wash and haircuts so long that I have been of which I highly recommend. ????

The local businesses after all we have supported me in my venture of Tom West's stories. So when you visit these places if you do. Please mention where you receive.

Tom West supporting local business.

A great big thank you also with many people on the Internet that has given me the support in helping me through my terrible grammar problems

Helen Summers. Bristol

Also a big thanks you to John Thornhill and his support.

My thoughts and memories to Marianne Thornhill who I dedicated this book too

RIP my good friend

I also dedicate this book to my father

RIP dad may you rest in peace.

This is my first fiction novel, I have thoroughly enjoyed meeting people and also writing this interesting story, I have had great enjoyment in every way. So there you go there is nothing more else for me to say except, please enjoy this fabulous story that has been influenced by the ideas of many people.

Many thanks to you all from.

Tom West the author.

CHAPTER 1

Standing in the darkest shadow veil of the Manor house doorway dressed in an unobtrusive grey parcel delivery uniform.

The morning sun is provoking to break through one of the most cloudy spring mornings this year. The sun breaks through the clouds now and then, revealing an obscure shadowy figure of a man or woman with long hair standing under the stone archway porch trying their best to enter the Manor house front door within a very surreptitious manner.

Struggling, muttering to oneself, "this blasted key does not fit!," double-time now, he is thinking and listening carefully to the lock's tumblers hearing that one or two are catching, as this key is slightly incorrect. Understandably he needs to be more belligerent with this stubborn blasted lock.

Abruptly forcing Forcibly, thrusting the key into the door lock, Once again: hitting it with the handle of his screwdriver at the same time, making the pins inside the door lock barrel jump. Knowing now that he needs to apply a lot more pressure on the key bumping the key once more. The Yale lock gives up its secrets as the brass pins soon line up correctly. Click! After one final turn of the key, the lock is now free to open with ease.

No scratches or visual damage to the lock to alert anybody of tampering.

I have already drawn out my iPhone to check the alarm code number that is displayed on my phone's photographs in the form of a photo-edited image preparing myself. With a quick glance from an untrained eye, you would see a few coloured dots. Have you ever experienced the colour-blind code test before? If you have then, you know what I mean. Double checking, memorizing the numbers 762 *4 the maintenance system, as I will just have one chance at this modern high-tech alarm, bypassing the biometric fingerprint recognition system in one step, this can only be possible with this maintenance code. Additionally, deep breath plus a slight pushes on the door. Smoothly silently, the door swings open.

Expeditious movements. First thing is to roll out this big rubber mat, thus giving me enough room to step inside the house as I am (against the clock?)on the clock as soon as the door opens time is ticking. Instantly rubbing my fingerprints off the door handle both sides in and out, as I am closing the solid oak door quietly behind me.

Visually I can determine that the alarm box is not by the entrance as described prolifically in the recce notes. Quickly pulling on the elasticated leather overshoes. Immediately after, then the right latex rubber glove wiggling my fingers to make the gloves fit snugly. That only takes a second, as I am very nimble. A good job is done dealing with this jobs research,' I can assure this with a few two quick strides down the hallway towards the alarm console right there in front of me. Quickly flicking open of the plastic cover with my forefinger, there is the key code keypad all lit up. No time to waste as the L.E.D starts to flash on the alarm console warning oneself that this alarm is about to trip and go off setting off all the sirens, just briefly before I am beginning to punch in the numbers seamlessly 762 *4. Immediately the alarm console L.E.D lights turn off.

"That was too close for comfort," big deep breathes and back to work

Then two nimble strides backwards to the oak door; inconstant smoothly calmly crouching down to my knees; rolling up this rubber matt languidly making sure that I catch all the bits in the roll, removing any chance or possibility of identifiable footprints left on the entry. Zipping this up securely!

Contiguous taking the other glove out of my pocket, quickly quietly as I'm pulling it onto the left hand. Silicon dust floats up into the sunlight that was beaming through this side door window at that moment. As I am silently listening for any movement before one precedes... it is nothing all clear. ??

Carrying on with the job at hand smoothly turning about unwaveringly on my haunches moving down onto all fours keeping as quiet as possible like a spider, avoiding making any shadows that may be cast against the stained glass windows at the end of the hallway therefore possibly revealing my silhouette to any of the gardeners whom (may?) would raise the alarm.

Down the corridor, the first on the left is the drawing room. Next, quickly like a marauding spider heading into that direction.

Taking the prone position and crawling over the highly polished slabs of white marble across the occasional black marble insert stretching along the hallway with my mouth widely open concealing the sound of my heavy breathing. Up to the drawing room door and threw onto the carpet, ongoing as a spider creeping silently into the drawing room on my fingertips and tiptoes.

After looking around the corner scanning the room at ankle, level guaranteeing there is no one in the room. Consistently using all human awareness.

Making sure any impressions in the carpet are removed with no hesitation. Soon I was standing up right tight against the wall. Feeling all the sinews and muscles akin in my body, as I rested for a brief moment concealed in the Shadows in the drawing room

A quick peep back into the hallway low around the door jam scanning any reflective surfaces to increase my visual range is most important.

Verifying a clear unseen entrance, All clear!

Quickly glancing down at the thick burgundy carpet. Looking at my distinctive fingerprint markings within the deep carpet pile. In an artless imaginative manner, unlike similar to stiletto shoes ????. If I were leaving these marks, "nobody would know would they?"

The house cleaners will be here approximately 2 o'clock, so I will have to remove these imperfections to make sure. A quick rub with my foot, to absolve this evidence. These cleaners are thorough and will be hoovering right through the Manor house, therefore, totally removing any evidence by the end of the Day. They will be starting their shift this afternoon.

There is one window in the drawing room, plus it occurs to be shaded by a tree. (, shaded by a tree) This prevents anyone look in easily into the drawing room.

I knew that it›s safe from prying eyes. So making it easy for oneself to work straight away. A car draws upon the next door's drive. Apparently knowing??? That this is a diesel. Bang on time I thought. One still has four hours concerning the owners of the house returning. Whilst looking around the room to see clear the gorgeous Goya painting. Hanging proud in its pride of place over the ornate fireplace.

Looking to my right near the grand piano, I can see the oak bookcase housing the drawers that I am looking for. As these drawers are my particular first interest. Standing upright walking quietly and comfortably over towards the oak bookcase containing the set of drawers. (At that moment?) This moment I could hear a car door slam shut. Beep! Beep! The noise of his alarm on the motorcar from the mansion next door.

Taking this Moment Looking for the second drawdown, one quick tug on the drawer handle finding out that it is locked.

Pick this quickly was no problem; I can do this with my eyes shut. Unzipping my paper overalls to open my inside jacket. Pulling out of the inside jacket pocket a skeleton key from my pocket. One other set that I have been collecting by purchasing antique furniture in the yesteryear. Instantly zipping up my paper overalls so to prevent any fibres from my jacket falling onto the carpet. This key completes the first turn, opening this draw lock smoothly. Moreover, seeing into the draw on the bottom stack of paperwork there is the document I am after for the Goya painting.

Kneeling down, to get hold of the rucksack off my back.

Pulling out the counterfeit parchment document of authenticity. Sliding the fake parchment documentation underneath the original papers of authenticity into the draw. At the same time smoothly extracting out the original paper. "Gently does it." Rolling this fragile verified parchment up carefully, then sliding the art treasure into the thin cardboard tube. Now placing this into my rucksack quicker. Presently it is time for the actual painting. Another few steps after closing the draw and making sure that everything is in its place. I am now making my way over towards the fireplace gingerly but carefully making sure that my footprints that will be remaining will not be seen so clear in the thick wool mix rich burgundy carpet.

That is easy enough, while one is taking each step smoothing the pile of the carpet as much as I can, therefore, taking my foot off the rug concealing my own footprints. The overshoes were designed to my specifics to help cover the pattern from the sole of my boots.

A few more strides over to the fireplace now standing right in front of the impressive antique Goya painting.

The man is the model posing in the portrait looking over his shoulder wearing a military uniform with a gold braid lanyard over his shoulder that is the ace!

Again, I took my rucksack off my back and placed it on the fire hearth avoiding any imprints in the carpet. This is what I am after.

This 18th-century painting looked astonishingly full of colour. The eyes of this picture seemed to be staring down at me watching my every move. On the other hand, is this just paranoia? As I am initiating to kneel down in front of the master under his cold piercing eyes glaring down at me from the painting.

Opening up my rucksack once more preparing for the surgical operation. Now instantly pulling out a large cardboard tube this would entirely be accommodated to the size of the masterpiece. Next now emptying the leather contents of the cardboard tube onto the carpet.

Then I rolled out the section of pigskin leather. Standing up and looked around the side of the painting in my little telescope mirror. Out of my pigskin leather tool roll that my wife had bought me the previous Christmas, "bless her cotton socks." I have rolled this out earlier beside the pigskin leather mat. Along with my mirror and torch, thoroughly checking for any alarm wires connected to the back of the painting.

However, there was nothing there.

This painting was just simply hung on a picture wire on the hawk over the picture rail. Gently putting the tools away placing my own inspection mirror, torch back into the tool roll bag. Soon standing up. In addition, with one quick sweep of my arm underneath the painting on the wall to verify that there is not anything that, I may have missed. Immediately firmly grasping hold of the picture frame painting. Next, gently lifted this heavy frame off its hook. I can feel my heartbeat as I finally had it in my hands, now placing the painting face down on the leather mat. So then I began to part the ageing brown paper with my scalpel gently away from the frame taking care not to cut the paper, as I went to work on the back of the painting. Removing the Goya from its frame, after gently removing the nails from the back of the frame that held it in place. Taking my time while doing this.

Notably, with a torch stuck firmly in my mouth, lighting the way to my workplace. One or two more nails to delicately remove making sure not to slip or scratch anything. Soon the painting is free from its frame. Carefully removing the top and bottom antique stretch bars from the antique canvas. Now I am starting to prepare the next wooden stretch frame that I made for this beautiful painting only last week. Proudly out of a very old wine box wooden crate these pieces of old timber were aged appropriately. Now skilfully quickly building these together the two stretch bars, checking the size of them against the original stretch frame. Soon after this next produced a second cardboard tube emptying the contents and then rolling out a freshly painted canvas From Wolfgang the artist who painted this only three months ago for my own personal commission. Tacking this together with rusty carpet tacks to the canvas and it's prepared frame. Then also stretching the canvas like an old drum skin. Matching the size of the frame with the top and bottom stretcher bars. Moreover, replacing the original painting with an artistic fake. A few more nails to place back in their holes and a dab of superglue to secure, we are done. Moreover, replacing the frame back on its Hook. I am quite proud of the artwork it looks just like the original. Also removing the two top stretcher bars from the original painting and rolled this up very neatly in one's protective soft leather pigskin mat. Moments later I had placed it snuggly all back safely in the cardboard tube. At that moment pushing the lid on nice and tight placing it back into the rucksack with the rest of my equipment that has been used. A quick look in the room to make sure that nothing is disturbed. It looks the same as it looked before. As if I was never there. A few more steps forward to the white marble floor with black granite inserts.

I went down quietly to my knees and stretched forward as I am attempting to do a couple of press-ups. So then, skilfully out of the doorway I crawled across the highly polished marble floor similar to a spider on my tiptoes and fingertips. Once again to avoid any silhouettes on the Windows so not to alert the gardeners to my presence as I'm crossing the long hallway to the alarm code box to reset the system

Soon calmly strolling towards the door looking towards the escape route. Peering through the spy hole in the oak door to make sure that everything was clear. Opening the door smoothly and stepping outside *quickly* removing the silicon gloves with my back towards the road and proceeded to stuff them safely away into my pocket. Soon I am calmly walking down the driveway in the shadows after locking the door behind. Quickly and quietly, I am jumping onto my foldaway mountain bike Getaway vehicle. Does one's children normally leave their pushbikes up against the garden hedge? Out of sight. Quickly cycling out garden to the getaway and out of the gates down the road unseen or noticed, blending into the environment like a chameleon.

I am very pleased with *myself* and enjoying the cycle ride *too*.

The whole manoeuvre only took 45 minutes. 5 miles to cycle back through the streets. Approximately 23 minutes soon after I arrived at my original location of a farmer's field on the outskirts of the town.

Cycling up to the edge of the road then picking up the mountain bike to prevent any dirt tracks in the soft mud on the approach to the gate lifting it over the gate once more. Quickly jumping over the large gate and carrying the bike on my shoulder 50 m into the field towards my concealed second getaway vehicle it is still there where I left it only 91 minutes ago. I pulled off the camouflage netting carefully not to damage anything. Folding my mountain bike up. Soon slipping it into the back of my microlight aeroplane along with my rucksack; then began pushing this microlight aircraft out into the open field. Starting the engine. This started first turn of the key; now I am accelerating into the middle of the freshly bailed cornfield getting my speed up; happily suddenly taking off. "Up, up and away!" a fantastic Scenery view, as I take off to the sky. The sky was clear as I am accelerating as I am climbing into the sky to 500 feet as fast as possible

I am flying approximately 100 miles towards my favourite golf course in St Andrews. The scenery is breath-taking knowing full well that I have got my prize in my rucksack of a good morning's work of 1.5 million profit approximately.

"Just in time for securing the alibi the last few imaginary holes on the golf course."

I brought the microlight down in his usual Private, secluded airstrip. He landed beautifully.

As one landed, Glenn Charlie's good friend of his was waiting for him. *Me?*

"*Hello Glenn,*" a smile and a wave from the cockpit. Moreover, then Glenn came running over to one's prize microlight when one rolled it to a stop and extinguished the engine.

Glenn said, "Hello Charlie"

Charlie replied happy to see his partner in crime, "Hello Glenn"

"You made it in good time then Charlie."

"Oh yes, the journey was quite uneventful. So therefore I managed to fly straight through with everything if you know what I mean."

"No problems there then Charlie."

As one started to unpack one's golf club bag from the back of the microlight. Placing in a couple of cardboard tubes, as they is speaking. "We need to hurry, as we are due on the golf course need to be on the course soon, as we are booked in." (With a wink and a smile) Here is your clubs Glenn. "Why thank you, sir" with a happy smile on his face. We both walked over to the car and swapped the golf bags. Thom asked, "is everything okay with the offence." Glenn replied. "Spiffing I do believe this is yours" and handed Charlie a nice fat brown envelope. One immediately opened up the envelope, nodded, smiled, and then stuffed the envelope into his jacket. They both shook hands and had a jokey joke between each other about the great game of golf they had earlier Glenn gave Charlie the Golf scoring card that was played earlier that day. Glenn said, "I am sorry to say, but you did not need to overdo :-) it. Thank you for the winnings Glenn." (Smiling to acknowledge Glenn) Charlie slips off his leather Overshoes and washes them under the tap. Then Charlie walks over to his microlight getting in and pulling the straps tight. Waving goodbye to Glenn. Charlie turns the key and starts the engine. Giving it time to warm up.

Glenn says, "I will be in touch," Then Charlie nodded and gave a salute.

Charlie starts taxing forward onto the runway and pushing the throttle open then taking off. Charlie flew smoothly straight up into the air to begin the long flight back to his home. Keeping his altitude, low for a few miles. (Underneath the radar)

CHAPTER 2

232, miles 189. 59° south as the crow flies heading towards Telford approximately 80 miles left to go, making good time with a strong tailwind. Supposing one is pushing the envelope a little bit high while flying within the limits of safety as high as one possibly can do without oxygen. Racing is a great mania to which one must sacrifice everything, without reticence, without hesitation. Racing just over the top of the clouds canopy within, this heavenly place.

among the cotton wool clouds delivering me the scenery of a flurry of white snowfall blankets. The crisp Warming sunshine is beaming into the cockpit from behind me. Warm-Hearted as the sun one just loves an incredible feeling here. There is nothing so free in this world as this sense of enamoured feeling of flying free above the rooftops of the world. The soft, supple drone of the engine as the prop screws its way through the air helping myself to one's final destination through the day as fast as possible with no traffic jams. Consequently, these 100 miles is a blast. As one's light aircraft is capable of 120 knots per hour. Fast approaching the edge of one's hometown just off to the right of the

Pennine Chain. There it is. Charlie recognise that hill as he fly is over his city. Smoothly turning looping back into the wind preparing to descend. Soon afterwards descending to an appropriate altitude. Flying and soaring in within this incredible agile microlight at an extremely low altitude. Hoping in some way or another, it would fool anybody trying to discover my Direction of from which one has just flown. A quick check on my GPS coordinates yes, that is okay ones on the correct heading. Straight over the top of the little church where a great friend of mine whom we miss dearly is buried there Marianne Thorn hill.

So now she is immortalised in my book God bless you, Marianne x. great place to leave secret messages. Pickup, Drop-off, Location, Times etc.

At Marianne's thorn hills place. If you ever visit her, please leave a good luck flower and a 1p piece.

Going back to the task for there is a considerable amount of turbulence over the town borders. So opening the throttle to give it more power. As there is nothing else, anyone really can do especially oneself while flying at a medium altitude towards the wrecking and around the hill making use of the dead ground cover. I am in sight of the 18th hole. This golf course is the epitome of all that is purely transitory from the air. A place, not to dwell in but to overcome! Quickly as possible. After the golf course taking the aircraft to a new low altitude across the fields for a few miles hedge hopping as a covert manoeuvre. Being especially careful not to spook the cattle. Soon approaching to land on my back garden field. Swiftly flying over the runway at first as a recce. Making sure that it is all clear to land and clear from obstacles our horses although they are trained rather well to keep clear,

but we need to give them a warning first. Within
of a flyby! Before landing on the runway in the field
a south easterly direction along the approach. Oak trees
pine trees each side of the field runway producing a shelter.
Avenue runway. Executing a steep bank turn around and
lining oneself up to the three° runway markers, as it is only
a grass field rolled regular. It can get quite slippery when
wet. Slightly bumpy in places, especially if you hit the soft
verge ground either side of the rolled grass runway. Flying
in on a rapid, steep dive furthermore then suddenly pulling
back on the stick, to level out. Keeping the wings inflated
on the landing approach is important. Now! Approximately,
12" inches from the ground. Then a thump and bump not
so smooth this time finally a touched down safely landed.
Decreasing the throttle power rapidly back to the taxiing
speed. Touching the brakes gently to reduce the speed down
the grass runway as gradual as possible, along the makeshift
grass runway. Also keeping an eagle eye out for my horse
while, coasting the aircraft straight towards the log cabin
horses stable shelter.

Pushing my key fob button once (click). The back of the
stables shelter opens up electronically. The double doors are
revealing the entrance of the secret double garage. Using
the ramp down to the subterranean entrance of the aircraft
hangar Bay. Now all one has to do is roll the microlight
down the ramp. As one does this with the keyfob once
more to close the door behind as the large double doors lock
clicked into place, the lights come on automatically. Safely
away within the microlight hanger. One's man cave. Even
my horse is pretty well-trained as he saunters in and starts
feeding on the hay saver slow feeder basket attached to the
back of the door. I can hear him sniffling and tugging on

the hay feeder. Hither gives one a warming welcome feeling inside, a lovely welcome home. My stallion horse Smith's snuffles at the door knowing that I am just the other side of the doors.

Knowing that I am home. This moment one quickly glances onto the CCTV monitor just to see if the coast is clear making sure that one had not received any unwelcome visitors in the day while we were all out. While I was picking up one's mobile phone off the charger on the desk. There happens to be on my phone 2 miss calls and one text message. A text message from the Mrs, "Enjoy your golf game today, gone shopping with the girls be back at 4 PM. Xxx :-) "She should be home in about 20 minutes. This insistence gives me plenty of time to be packed away and cleaned up. The next message, a coded message from Josh., "Hello, Charlie we will see you on the golf course at 9:00 AM." Something as plain and simple as that to Covers my alibi.

An average game of golf takes about four hours, so approximately 1 o'clock is the rendezvous time. Move to the next message phone call from the Surgery. "Good fortune. With your wife's art exhibition on Friday, we will be there, thank you very much for your invitation to this amazing Art exhibition." (The answering machine speaks a robot part.) "Press one to listen to this message again. Pressed two save the message. Press 3 to delete the message." Beep. Pressing number three on the mobile phone Screen. Leaving the one important message from Josh about the golf game. Next importantly proceeding immediately to refuelling the microlight. With my new powered fuel pump as you commonly experience at any petrol station. Here I installed over half dozen months ago. Is not this just the best thing since sliced bread making the task so much quicker easier to do? It just saved me so much time in the daylight. Instead of messing around with Jerry cans. Besides, then presenting a general servicing to the engine, checking the oil on the dipstick. "That is all right." Changing the microlight numbers on the registration board on the wings and tail and then filling in my pilot's log to correspond with the hours also flown enforcing one's alibi. The next little job to do is taking out my foldaway mountain bike from the back of the micro light. Then giving this a speedy clean up. After it is sparkling hanging it, back up on the stand next to the microlight. Taking out my little cordless Hoover and giving the microlight interior a very intense clean. Subsequently emptying the contents of the Hoover bag, into a plastic bag with my silicone latex gloves and mobile phone chip. That I used earlier that day Along with the microlight registration numbers instantly tucking the bag into my pocket. After tying this bag up nice and taut. Removing my Grey paper overalls and folding them up placing them into another plastic bag, I suppose my O.C.D is getting a little over obsessive. However, I just imagine it will save my life one day.

Then proceeding to remove the golf clubs bag and rucksack from the microlight. Opening the first draw in the desk halfway. Then pushing the second draw entirely into the desk carcass (click it operated as the mechanisms located each other) additionally pushing a lever underneath the desk slightly to the left hand side. Instantly unlocking the mechanical locks in the correct sequence. Then pulling the corner of the desk, which easily swings this open on hinges? Half of this office desk will only come away from the wall to reveal a secluded concealed opening, within the wall behind the desk draw cases. So then one immediately place this rucksack/grab bag back into the secret space. Then pushing the desk back closing the concealed compartment with the desk. Thoughtfully returning the draw to its place fully closed. Suddenly putting the two plastic pedal bin bags into my golf bag. Additionally, Giving Josh A-1 Ring dropped call signal from my phone. That sends a message to Joshua saying that I am home and safe. Josh Confirmed, he will now send a radio broadcast to the airport Airways asking aircraft clearance to take off from the private airstrip. Important for logging my air registration, call sign to the tower. After this, putting my mobile phone in my top pocket. Proceeding to walk to the next exit and pull the light cord in the hallway that is taking me to the garage. Lighting up the long secret subterranean corridor. So now, I am running down the hall underground towards my Garage up one flight of steps striding the steps two at a time to a steel door entering into the garage behind a large Snap-On Toolbox. First checking everything was clear through the CCT in the garage. Stepping into this room through another concealed doorway. Into the car Garage, Walking past, a pair of his and her pride and joy Motorcycles BMW S1000RR. Standing their pride of place in the garage next to our black Mercedes-Benz remained parked. Taking the Mercedes car keys off the hook and pressing the button opening up the boot of my Mercedes-Benz. I removed the golf clubs from my shoulder and place them gently in the boot of the car and removing the plastic bags putting them in my pocket. Then taking out the brown paper package from my shirt multitasking closing the boot of the car at approximately the same time. Turning around walking to the back wall of the garage pushing in a breezeblock in the wall. Next walked over to the left hand side of the garage and opened a long draw in the cabinets. The draw rolled out in sections. Placing the brown paper package filled with the money that Josh had given me earlier that day for my hard work. So sliding the drawer shuttle closed. Hearing a clunk as the cash dropped into a biometric safe behind the workbench. As the draw closed the breezeblock along the wall popped back into its place. I reopened this draw just to confirm my actions are completed. Moreover, the safe is locked. All that was in the draw was a few papers and a spare key, but the draw would not open any further, and now I have closed it again. My mobile phone started to Vibrating and made the sound of a car engine. Within my top pocket, for half a second as it normally does. Especially when this draw is being or has been opened without the correct combination, this will also activate the concealed CCTV cameras in the garage on my phone. Also making sure that the draw is firmly closed. Casually walk over to the door and then opening the side door to the hallway leading into the house from the garage. Walking up the stairs and placed my keys on the table. Accordingly, walked over to the coffee machine and personally made a nice hot coffee drink. Also thoughtfully prepared a cup and cartridge of coffee, so it is already from my wife, Helen. All she has to do is to push my button to get a hot fresh one. "I am sure she is going to appreciate this when she comes back in a few minutes. From her shopping trip with the ladies," saying this one while wiping the site down with a dry cleaning cloth. Thinking about the hot one that I am going to give her.

A quick sit down for a few minutes while I enjoy the newspaper and my cup of coffee. Realizing a bulging my trousers know it was not my cock this time it was the two plastic bags I must get free of these. Hence, I stood up and walked into the garden to the barbeque. Placed the two bags into the barbecue furthermore covered them with some charcoal with the firelighters. Immediately lighting the grill with my brass Zippo. I do not smoke anymore, but the brass Zippo is a souvenir from the past. The flame from my Zippo buffeted slightly in the wind, so I shielded it with my right hand, soon the flames caught on the firelighters, and a nice steady fire grew. Getting the barbecue ready and hot. Furthermore destroying any evidence. Then walked back to the house and sat back down in my comfortable chair, taking another sip out of my coffee cup. Choosing some appropriate background easy listening music from my iPhone. Several moments later, a car pulls up in the driveway. It is Helen, my lovely wife. Then I stood up and casually walked over to the coffee machine. So prepared a hospitality drink for my wife. Hot drink. Ready for when she strolled in through the doorway. Therefore, I endured there for a moment waiting in anticipation for her to walk through the door. (Beep) The alarm is set on her car the front door opens and in walks my wife carrying an assortment of designer labelled bags. I instantly believed that she had been to the mailbox in Birmingham. A fabulous figure or physique is nice, but it is self-confidence that makes someone extraordinarily sexy. She greeted me with a brilliantly white smile as she walks in through the doorway. "Hello, dear." I immediately stepped forward and said, "Would you like a hand with these dear."

Taking the Baggies out of her hands, but she kept hold of one little Dusty pink bag also but would not let me take it.

"It is a surprise." Then she leaned forward and paid me a greeting kiss. Every time my dear does that, i could just melt inside. We both strolled into the house and set the large bags down on the living room coffee table. The little bag that she was carrying she seemed to cherish. So temptingly, she kept looking at oneself and looking at the bag. "did you have a good day honey on the golf course?"

"i have had a very entertaining day, thank you very much, love. Would you like coffee?"

"you are such a sweetie, yes, please, honey."

My baby follows me into the kitchen still carrying this little pink paperback. In addition, she places it on the kitchen island while I prepare her coffee. I could tell that she was smiling with excitement and kept peeking into the bag to entice me to be more inquisitive. I poured the coffee and walked around the island still looking into her eyes carrying a coffee. The anticipation of this parcel was growing. I placed the coffee cup and saucer onto the island and slid close to her. "Would you like to see what it is Charlie?" I love it the way she says my name. "Yes please," she flutters her fingers over the top of the back as if she is a magician, but also still looking into my eyes. Then she glances down and slowly slips her slender fingers deep inside the pink bag and pulls out a leather blindfold. My eyes light up one lean forward to give her a kiss with passion. The warm feeling of her lips on mine for a few moments "Oh no you must wait you naughty boy" and once again she enters her pink paperback with her exquisite French manicure. "Wait," she smiles. And holds her hand in their four in anticipation. And slowly pulls out a second blindfold.

"Oh yes" with a smile "we have been only just talking about that last Saturday afternoon.

"I know I saw them in the shop I could not wait to get them back home to try them out." With this excited hire pitch in her voice. Then daintily and she picks her coffee cup up and takes a sip. One knows that bag is not empty; I could tell that the way she was guarding it and building the anticipation of a secret.

"Thank you for my incredibly exciting present."

Oh what honey sweetheart,

"Yes baby cakes."

"It is not all over yet you know honey,"

"You mean there is more."

"Oh yes baby you are the best man in my life, and I want to show you my appreciation" another glance down to the bag and she finally pushes the Pink bag towards me. It was heavy I could see the way It moved. An expression of delight adorned her beautiful face.

This is not very often I get excited at this moment I was.

"O my dear love you should not have. " I picked the little pink bangle bag by the handles and it was rather heavy I could not imagine what it is going to be. I could see Helen's face staring at me holding her hands together with excitement and one of those fabulous smiles that can melt me on the spot.

Therefore, I placed my hand deeply into the pink. Suggested a long Sling box inside. I wrapped my fingers around it, and then pulled on it until it popped out.

I can feel my heart beating. (Bump. Bump, Bump.) One felt the weight of it. What is this? The box was black with a gold crown interesting insignia on. It was definitely heavy. This moment as much as I possibly could. Gently with my fingertips, I played with it to find the opening. Then sure enough it popped open. "Oh, my dear it is beautiful, so big and so powerful looking."

"I knew you would love it."

Said, "darling it is the finest that I have ever seen and what I have always wanted" they hot and passionate kiss over the island we could not put each other down. However, I had to resist.

"It is beautiful is not it."

Softly she says, "oh yes honey oh yes." and puts her hand in the box and strokes it on my cheek.

"Baby, can I try it."

"Yes, of course, it is yours," :-)

The feel of it was so smooth but also like silk in your hand. Isolated old onto my wrist and then closed the Clasp of my brand-new Pearl Oyster Rolex. This watch. Is definitely a welcome sight? I will certainly be proud to have this on my arm as well as my lovely caring wife.

CHAPTER 3

"Honey, I want to get a shower. And then we can have a decent barbecue in the garden." Helen takes another long sip from her coffee cup. "That will be superb for tonight. It will give us time to sort out the transcriptions for my Friday night art exhibition." Charlie pulls the stakes out from the fridge and places them on a plate to rest before cooking. "Stakes are always better rested do you not think so dear," Charlie's wife replies with a smile. (At the same time Helen starts to thumb through a glossy magazine on the kitchen island and ends quickly at an attractive page and looks at the painting art exhibition, advertising) In addition, asks, "Dear do you think they have done a good job of the advertising," smoothly she brushes her long dark brown hair back behind her ear. Looks over the island towards her husband shortly waiting in anticipation for a reaction. Charlie closes the electric refrigerator door and walks over to his woman. Furthermore comfortingly sits down next to her on the stool at the end of the island. Put is his fingertips on the edge of the magazine and his muscular arm around her tiny waistline and looks and studies the article carefully for a long while.

"It is very well written and a great advert the headline combines a powerful benefit toward your advertising. Yes, one likes it very much honey I am very proud of you. I received this text message today and the young women from the office have accepted your invitation to your art exhibition on Friday. They seem excited about it all. One senses it is proceeding to be a big hit, honey. As everyone seems to be excited and speaking about it." " Thank you, Charlie, you say such lovely words, I love you so much." " You are my amazing woman and I love you so much, what can go wrong these days." " That is a really lovely painting" as Helen turns the page. In addition, reads out the following article on the page with interest.

Without Prejudice, With Newtown Galleries.

From who purchased this via, the Harvey family? The Estate of Mrs. Rrnestine R. Harvey and the Westgate of R. Stanton Harvey (sold to benefit the R. Stanton Harvey Foundation), London auction house, 22 May 1990, lot 164, of £220,000. CATALOGUE NOTE Isaac's wintertime landscapes were a Specialty of his repertoire, which consisted mostly of natural interiors and outdoor panoramas. He painted wintry appearances from 1641 throughout a fleeting profession since satisfied barely a decade until his last at the age of twenty-eight. Most, related the contemporary work, are composed of an inclining Community also adopt a little viewpoint across an expanse of frozen. This white charger, which here emphasizes in the middle ground, was a favourite theme. The crisp lines and shadings in this excellent example, extract the similar handling of his greatest drawings. An inferior account of this painting that reproduces the principal constituents of the composition in the oval arrangement was sold in these Opportunities as the range of Isaac van

Octave. Responsibility of which was mentioned earlier. Which remains unrecorded against the examination? Once compared toward the art biographer Otto Muddler (1811–70), whichever represented as an attorney-at-law for the National Museum in London throughout the second half of the 1850's." Charlie talks under his breath, to himself. "Wolfgang"

"Pardon."

"No, it is all right, dear, I was just expressing out loud." "Okay, are you going to jump in the shower now?" "Yes, honey I will. Then we can settle in for the evening." Next Charlie Leaves his wife in the kitchen Reading the magazine as Charlie walks out the kitchen. Through the living room into the hallway and up the stairs. Charlie was chuckling to one's self, thinking about the painting that his wife had just read the article about. As it had managed to be sold by the auction for such a profit and Charlie knew it was a fake as only three months ago he had changed it. He also knew who the forgery artist was his name was Wolfgang.

Before long, Charlie is in the shower room undressing, throwing his clothes in the linen basket. Turning the music up in the bathroom from the surround sound household entertainment system. Almost involuntarily, he turned on the shower. He can indeed feel the goose bumps on one's skin. As if one's own skin is awakened from the exhilarating, refreshing shower water warming up. A quick squeeze of the shampoo bottle to release this content into one's own hand. Standing underneath the Showerhead for a bit to whet his hair. Then stepping out of the powerful water to use the luxurious refreshing shampoo on his hair. The heavenly heaven shampoo bubbled up in a thick lather and rolled down my chest, giving out a pleasant, sweet fragrance while one was washing their long hair. The soapy lather bubbles roll down over every muscular contour of one's own body so refreshed. As the force of the water is beating on my body instantly, removing these aches and pains away with the power of this life-giving water. Grabbing some more heaven body wash scrubbing my chest and testicles and cock to make sure that my manhood is spotlessly clean. Now it is time to shave off all body hair clean the way. At this moment whilst stretching one's own cock to begin shaving it clean. He can feel a sudden change of air pressure in the room, the same breeze you get when a door open has and closes again. Nevertheless, this did not concern Charlie for the security and safety of his own home. Knowing that it can only be his wife joining him in the bathroom. With what he was, doing so Charlie finished shaving his body. Turning around in the shower to wash off the soapsuds. There, standing in front of oneself was an unexpected sexy surprise. A beautiful hot figure of a woman, standing with her legs apart in a domineering position with knee length leather boots sexy fun, sheer, flirty Babydolls Lingerie Panties. Wearing a blindfold just standing there as still as a statue... Not moving an inch, as if she is a piece of art. In her right hand, holding a long black leather whip slowly naturally rolling out from her hand like a leather snake uncoiling onto the floor in silence.

Drowned out by the sound of this shower water happens to be identical to Heavy tropical rain pounding on my body. Still she stood there still like a statue. Becoming instantly Aroused. Deciding to put the Bike razor down back on the shelf to be safe. Moving quietly within the dominant noise of the shower. I could understand that my wife is feeling powerful as she was there blocking the exit of the shower there was no way to escape. I could see straight through the baby doll top that was barely covering the breasts. The steam was starting to envelop the room, as I found my eyes fixed and entrenched onto her nipples, as I could see the areola twisting as she was getting more aroused. In addition, the music played on "Ooh La" by Goldfrapp Sometimes you just want to get it on without all the responsibilities. Is this what shower booty calls are for? —Marley Lynch, as her nipple pops totally wrecked. This was like a light switch turning on the sex drive. Then this leather-blindfolded woman impatiently cracked the whip. (Crack!) With one quick, powerful, fluid, fast movement. Instantly moving out of the way from the mighty leather whip. Stepping forward as close as one possibly could to my blindfolded kinky sexual predator. Flicking my hair at the same time, the beads of water flew through the air in an arc splashing onto her face. As she cracked the whip once more in quality of being insubordinate and disobedience to lawful authority then she squatted down on the floor with a growl of aggression and submission. I grabbed her long hair. Holding her head back far enough to proffer her to open her mouth as she said, "give it to me" without hesitation I struck my wet cock across my wife's face. She took a gasping breath, from the shock of the mighty stroke influencing across her face. She did not realise how hard and powerful. I was to be with her. As she brought her manicured nails like talons and thrust them into my behind inappropriateness is further squeezing hard. "Right! Kinky bitch you are definitely having it now." Charlie Paul back and grabbed his potent hot rod in his right hand then thrust it into her lips deep into her full mouth without hesitation. Even harder, she grabbed her husband's buttocks and pulled him in to choke herself. I could feel my ball sack tighten up, as the thrill and erotic power envelops my body. I just decided to let her go to work on my cock you could clearly see that she loved it as the lips caressed it tightly. She grabbed hold of it with her left hand, continued to suck and lick as if she was a starved animal relentlessly with no compassion except to feast on my cock. The power of this emotion ripples through Charlie's body as he was standing there in the shower being fed upon by his wife erotic animal instinct. Gorging on his manhood. With her relentless feasting. Sucking it in a factual manner deep into her throat as she does. Choking herself, repeatedly rhythmically moving faster and faster. Oh so hot, so rampant as the constant motion of her tongue and lips Work within perfect atonement with each other. Giving Charlie the pleasure of a Deep Throat that he so addicted to her thrusting powerful movements, I do not want this to stop. A sudden sharp, searing pain shoots off across my back. As the leather, whip strikes and bites me making an impact to his back setting off the adrenaline regarding pain and emotion. Still not giving in.

Still holding on tight. While my wife's power of her lips grew bounteous to the point of being uncomfortable. She began multitasking unzipping her long leather boots one at a time while still gorging on her husband's cock. The vision of her hand sliding down this seem of the zip pulling the zip down of her boots to her ankle slowly was so powerful to me. Charlie could not bear it any longer as he was watching his kinky wife unzip her long knee height black leather boots, this mighty shaft from his balls began throbbing with her smooth lips inspecting every part of his tightly stretched Lancing helmet.

A striking whip across the back certainly enhances feelings, so one grabbed a passing chance and ripped the whip out of her hand. Instantly forcing her face down between his thighs. Smacked her Buttocks with the handle of her own powerful whip. A little, whimper of passion emanated from her while she was on her hands and knees on the marble floor of the shower. Next grabbing my own, hot throbbing cock and held it tight to enhance the sensation of this horny feeling that one received moments before. While looking down upon my wife on the floor, panting for more while she seductively pulls her boots off. Passionately grabbing her by the waist picking her up. Up upside down with her legs over my shoulders, immediately started to gorge on her sweet, juicy bits. Ripping her thong off with my teeth and plunging my tongue deep into her wet and juicy cooch. While in the inverted 69 position, the shower is still raging as the full power of the water is cascading down. Just thinking with no consequences it was a good idea to take her upside down under the shower pounding that little clitoris with my tongue at the same time as the water power intensely pounded onto her bunny hole. I just love it when wet. It did not take her long to find her best friend as she pushed it into her mouth once more. Her heartbeat is strong one could tell she was enjoying it from the sensations she was giving me and I was giving her. This is the yin and yang of a relationship, to be able to work together in any situation. Especially when I am popping her nub. It is so hard within one's lips including on one's tongue, at the same time massaging her mons pubis with one's own chin. One can feel her wrecked clitoris against one's own chin as one does while working relentlessly to the pleasure as one does endure onto one's own horny erotic bitch. Still flicking her sexy hot nub with my tongue. Carrying her out from underneath the shower, the feel of her upside down in my arms as she moans loudly. The scent plus taste and gorgeous juicy sweet flavours that suddenly squirt into my mouth and one's face in bright jets of her hot cum juice. As she bites in passion down on my cock with in desire. So one slapped her hard on the cheeks of her arse with the handle of the leather whip. Just to gain a little bit of control! In the midst of passion. This just drove her furthermore wild. She screams out, "I want you inside me" Charlie spun her around in the air as if the woman was as light as a feather. Next, he removes the blindfold as she wrapped her legs around his waist her eyes fluttered like butterflies, as they grew accustomed to the light out of the darkness. She instantly started to kiss passionately rapidly and intensely. Charlie felt her warm lips of her labia majora kissing the tip of his cock. Charlie excitedly begins to penetrate a bit at a time. She stops kissing him and looks straight into her lover's eyes; Charlie looks straight back deep into her eyes and soul as her mouth opens into the passion. Only taking one swift moment and grab her buttocks in his hands pulling them open so he could get in with his fingers, playing with her labia and stimulating oneself at the same time. Something to bring higher than the senses as Charlie smoothly pushes his cock deeper inside of her pink taco.

A mixture of passion and pain. I can see it in her eyes. Then Charlie held her tightly as she also held on tight to Charlie's muscular, athletic frame, knowing what was about to come next. With one quick long thrust deep up inside of her I ploughed my throbbing cock into her hot bunny hole and rhythmically pounded out a tune of love into a hot passionate pussy. As he carried her out of the bathroom. Into the bedroom; threw her on the bed still deep inside of her. "There was no escaping as the passion and excitement excelled to a higher level as we both get really foxy with each other. The sweat was beading up on her face as we both buck and ride together rhythmically on the bed. Charlie pulls out his cock from her pink taco and rubs the end of his cock fast on the top inside of her G-spot juicy pussy. Harder and harder, he does this under her pubic bone. In addition, faster and faster. She starts to grab hold of the beds pillows everything that she can get her hands on at the same time destroying the bed. Then suddenly with a whimper she cries out. "No! No! Fuck me!" As the juices flow from her body, Charlie thrusts his already deep cock in as far as she would allow him nudging her cervix enough to heighten within the sensation. Passionately proceeds to fuck her with power as he builds up to his own climax. "Oh baby" intensely he steps up a gear. Riding his wife into ecstasy as his balls are about to explode he can feel his self-filling up. The powerful energy from the hormones that are released through his testicles enters his body, energy is released, and now we are on overdrive. Charlie gasps for breath as the sweat drips off his nose. The hot steaming bodies of the two love makers in perfect harmony are exactly where they want to be. Then Charlie pulls his cock out of her. Next thoughtlessly, Charlie grabs his wife's hair guiding her head towards his pulsating cock plus he pushes his cock into her mouth and shoots his hot cum juices filling the wife's mouth and face. With both testicles thoroughly emptied. Of which normally she would be happy with this. However, today for some reason it was different and you can clearly see that she was quite upset. For not receiving his seed. Charlie tried to console Helen by cuddling up to her in the best possible way he could. Even though the moment of passion had given way. The reasons Charlie could not quite understand but having the idea of this she was ready for a baby. Countless discussions before Charlie had said that he was not ready for a child until we are exactly where we want to be. These are difficult times when a couple needs to think as one and the timing is not quite right. Still Charlie gave his wife a cuddle and tried to console her crying. Tearfully she said could you make oneself a cup of tea. He gave Helen a Kiss and then walked out of the bedroom feeling rotten towards oneself. Then refreshing oneself with a quickly ran under the shower. Next grabbing a towel also his favourite dressing gown next walked out of the bathroom downstairs and into the kitchen. There on the kitchen Centre Ireland was the two stakes. Charlie turned on the kettle and prepared some oven-ready chips in the Aga.

Before this putting on his dressing gown on and carrying the plate of stakes out into the garden placing the steaks along the grill over the hot coals on the barbecue. Carefully replacing the lid covering the two sizzling steaks. He proceeded to walk back into the kitchen and finished making his wife a cup of tea. Soon after, he carried this upstairs into the bedroom and gave it to his wife.

"I have started dinner,"

"Really," she said (just giving Charlie a little bit of punishment for what he had thoughtlessly done earlier)

"Yes. There is your tea honey."

"Thank you, love Thank you" with a hint of sarcasm.

"Are you coming down with me now because the stakes are on the barbecue?"

"Yes honey, Lead the way! :-)" Helen stands up from the double bed with a cup of tea and walks to the window, and then proceeds to gazed out.

Charlie walks forward and gives his wife a soothing cuddle from behind her at the window as they both look out to the burning barbecue. "We must go down now else the stakes will be ruined."

"Come on let us go then, honey." Helen grabs hold of Charlie's hand and escorts him out of the bedroom down a flight of stairs through the living room and then on through the kitchen and outside. To the barbecue. Where Charlie gives Helen a lovely kiss. It did not take long for her to respond as soon as Charlie had her back on his side. "Sit down honey and drink your tea I am going to get the chips and plates." Helen walked towards the table and sat down. Moments afterwards, Charlie was back in the garden with everything that he needs to have a lovely enjoyable meal with his wife. Then he proceeds to lay out the table.

Charlie leans over the table. Lighting the two slim table candles with his Zippo lighter to set the mood on the table.

The golden colour of the flames shines brightly delicately lighting the table up as the flames grow. Helen says, "Thank you, they look so lovely." As Charlie walks over to the barbecue with the two hot plates with a portion of freshly cooked chips on each plate. With the tongues, he scoops up the freshly cooked steaks and places them on the plates. "Thank you, honey." "You are very welcome dear it is one's own pleasure to serve you" Helen has a very charming smile on her face, as she was very pleased being looked after so well by her husband. Charlie sits down and joins his wife at the table. Helen waited for a moment in anticipation while Charlie settled at the table. Helen pours the peppercorn sauce over her stake. She says, "Thank you, honey."

"What for?"

"Why that is natural honey just for being my husband."

"Oh, that is so kind of you Helen, I love you very much. I would not want to change you for the world."

Charlie cuts into his steak also the juices look the perfect colour. "Marriage is a lifetime for love and you are my love for my lifetime."

"Yes on our own wedding day, the vows reflected this. One could see this in you, Helen. You are not going to enter into a proposal or contract of marriage light-heartedly with oneself. One could also see that you are tremendously head over heels in love with your husband to be. One is with you, my dear.

"It's astonishing how we will be coupled in marriage for. Ten, fifteen, twenty, thirty, or even 60 years plus years and still find there remains much more together we don't know about each other.

Alternatively, so the experts say it is because modern marriages have lost the art of conversation.

Others say it is because couples do not allow it to continue after we marry we let the ordinary living intervene and indifference us alternatively.

Anything the case, it is none-the-less important to keep the lines of communication and conversation open so we grow together most assuredly than apart. Honey we are not going to allow ourselves to get into that sort of situation like that."

"Are we? So now can you tell oneself dear is there anything on your mind that may be troubling you?"

(A silence over the table as Helen is chewing on a piece of delicious peppercorn steak.)

Helen patted the corner of her mouth with her napkin and swallowed.

Charlie cut into a piece of his stake, placed it in his mouth, and started to eat it.

Helen says, "the only thing on my mind at the moment honey is how delicious your stake is you cook so well."

(In Charlie's thoughts. "So why did she get so upset? After romping session. I swear she wants a baby and I am not ready for it yet. Maybe she knows this and she just protecting my feelings. Alternatively, even to save an argument. Okay, time to take notice.")

Charlie looks over at his wife. As he is eating his delicious peppercorn steak. Then placing his hand on her leg, at the same time giving his wife a graceful smile to thank her for the compliment of the meal. Charlie and Helen have this gift to be able to communicate with each other without actually having to speak. However, sometimes things can be misled within their silent conversation. Charlie swallows and says, "Are you worried at all about the art exhibition dear?"

"Honey, not at all, one has everything in place the painters and decorators have finished everything inside and the floor is being laid this evening. I will be taking my art into the gallery tomorrow to be hung."

"Dear, it sounds like you have everything perfectly in order."

"Oh yes honey I do. And thank you very much for putting the painters and decorators in contact with oneself."

"You are dear, welcome anything to do to help you. You are such a courageous businesswoman and you have my full support, my darling."

"Dear, would you like a glassful of wine?"

"Honey that would be so beautiful we could treat ourselves to a nice red to complement the state, although bring a bottle I fancy a drink."

(Charlie wipes his napkin across his mouth, stands to uplift his chair up slightly whilst pushing the chair backwards silently making room for one. Then flamboyantly he places his white cotton napkin neatly over his arm, as he is standing up straight as if a trained professional wine waiter would.)

"It is a celebration so it commands the best!"

Charlie looks into his wife's eyes. She smiles excitedly Charlie then leaned forward from the waist giving one's own wife a kiss as she also responds with her romance.

Charlie walks off and disappears down some stairs in the garden. Helen could hear the key code from the wine cellar door also the door creaking open. So while her husband is in the basement. She goes out into the kitchen to get some glasses from the cabinet. Returning to the table just in time as her husband returns from the wine cellar, carrying a large oak box. Looking very pleased with himself before he places it on the table.

Charlie says, "Do you remember that ice hockey player?"

((While he is placing the wine casket on the table gently.))

"Which one honey?"

"You know that professional ice hockey player that decided to collect Wines and art. He said to you how fantastic your art is."

"Oh yes I remember now, he did have very nice eyes. (A sweet sexy teasing smiles from his wife.)

Mario Lemieux!

Of course dear one definitely remembers."

"But do you remember the little gift he gave us for our wedding gift a very special bottle of wine that we have kept just for a special occasion. Of your first exhibition. Of which we are going to celebrate this evening." (Charlie strokes one's hand over the top of the oak box with the cast iron legs feeling the craftsmanship with his sensitive fingers. Helen looks on in anticipation, as Charlie is about open the box.)

"Honey, this wine box is so beautiful. What is it made from?"

"Solid oak and cast-iron. Is not it not just a fabulous piece of artistic design in its own right?"

(Charlie pushed on the top of the lid. When opened this there was a beautiful bottle of wine nestled in the velvet-lined case. Showing a black and gold label. However also in there was a letter in a tiny envelope with these simple words saying." to my friends." wrote beautifully with calligraphy handwriting. (Helen leaned forward and looked further into the box) "What is the name of the wine?" Charlie grabs a napkin, rolls it around his hand, tucks the one corner of the napkin in to make a perfect funnel shape, and then stands the bottle up holding it very carefully within his hand. Then placed the napkin around the neck of the bottle. "There we've given a little tuxedo to the bottle of wine." Helen laughed as she was getting rather excited over this unusual bottle of wine. "What is the name of it?" (Charlie picks up the bottle and reads the label aloud whilst bringing it close to the candlelight.) The gold letters on the label sparkled shining the reflection from the flame from the table candles. "Chateau Margaux 2009 Balthazar!" Helen says, "What a lovely name for a bottle of wine. A fabulous read and label."

Charlie says,"I am scared of opening it." Helen picks up the two glasses and places them right next to her. "Come on honey I want to see you pour it." Charlie opens up the one side of the oak case and in there was a small bone handled knife and a matching traditional French corkscrew. "They both look timeworn" as Charlie, remarked. "These look old," Helen said, "possibly antique."

"Well, one's going to have to be very careful opening this wine is not one." Charlie takes out a knife and gently cuts off the top of the wax seal revealing the Cork. Then picks up the French corkscrew. Holding the bottle correctly furthermore tightly. Charlie turns the screw into the cork. In addition, gives it a good stronger mighty pull. Pop! Goes

the Cork. A clear and crisp pop! The aroma from the wine
fragrance wafted into Charlie's nose from the bottle. Charlie
then offered the Cork and the corkscrew to his wife, of
which she took from his hand. In addition, sampled the
fruity fragrance of the wine on Cork. "So good so far."
Charlie pouring a little measure into the bottom of the
glass taking care to twist the bottle to save any drips at the
same time. One's wife to taste. As she is taking a small sip
from the glass. Her full lips look so pale in comparison to
the red wine under candlelight, this full-bodied red wine.
You can see the enjoyment on Helen's face as she sampled
and tasted the incredible châteaux 2009 Baltazar. Helen
waited for a moment swirling the crystal glass in her hand.
The red wine whirl like a whirlpool in the glass. Spinning
up the sides of the wine glass as she watches it settle by the
candlelight. She could see the legs appear rolling down the
side of one's crystal as the flavours in her mouth mature
while she mixes them with the air by gently breathing in
through her pouting sexy lips.

"That is perfect honey." Charlie proceeded to pour his
beloved wife a full glass of a full-bodied red wine. Then
Charlie poured oneself a glass of the finest red wine. Before
tasting it. Charlie raised his glass. In addition, said these
words. "You are my love Helen, you are my whole world. We
will go far together. Even after our 60th wedding anniversary
my love will stay active in one's own heart as one am sure
it will be in your thoughts and heart also." To the future of
art and happiness" the two happy people husband and wife
chinking glasses and drinking to their future. Charlie says,
"Wow this wine is impressionable it is blooming gorgeous."
(Raising his glass as if he is saluting together with Helen. To
their good friend.) Saying his name aloud "Mario Lemieux

we salute you" Charlie then sits down in one's chair and snuggled close to his wife. Drinking also chatting through the evening enjoying this beautiful wine together. Helen leans forward and whispers into Charlie's ear, "I love you x" Charlie responds to her with a passionate embrace showing his love to his wife in a physical manner. The few minutes pass in the garden of dreams as this romantic couple are enfold together in perfect harmony. Charlie takes another sip of this gorgeous, delicious red wine.

He says, "Remember the letter within the wine bottle case box. I will get it if you can read it Honey." Charlie leans over the table just in his reach and manages to pick up the letter. In addition, presents it to his wife with both hands showing the inscription on the tiny envelope. "To my friends." Helen takes a letter and looks into Charlie's eyes. "Thank you, honey" with a pleasing smile of excitement. Helen gently takes the letter and breaks the little wax seal on the back of the tiny envelope. The envelope Seal pops open revealing a single card with an oyster shell edge upon it. Helen slowly pulls the card out from the envelope and begins to read the words.

"To my artistic friends Charlie and Helen,

Like a good wine-colour, a great love will deepen and mature with age.

Kind regards
Mario Lemieux."

Helen says, "That is just so perfect does one think, so honey?"

"The timing and diction of Mario it is just sublime. What a man."

Charlie and Helen clinking their glasses together said together "Mario Lemieux. May you live long and prosper with love in your heart."

Charlie looks straight into his wife's eyes and says, "I love you, and my dear, and I love you with all my heart." Helen responds by touching Charlie's face gently with her hand. While looking deeply into his eyes, "you are my rock baby." In addition, leans forward and starts kissing her sexy romantic husband. The passion grows within the garden and two consenting married adults KISS and drinks to their hearts content until the late evening within the glorious surroundings of their beautiful garden.

The candles are burning brightly and a lovely couple are enjoying their evening together. "Honey, how is the wine?"

"It is divine Charlie and very smooth, we have certainly got a good bottle here."

"I totally agree." Helen raises a glass and presents it to Charlie.

As if she was enticing Charlie to fill her glass up once again. Charlie took this moment and reached over the table, pulling the bottle out of the ceramic wine cooler. In addition, tops his wife's glass up to about 1 inch below the rim. Then proceeds to top up his own glass up to the same level as his wife. They both sit there quietly enjoying their wine. As the evening rolls on two approximately 11 o'clock.

Charlie says, "So honey, how many paintings do you have for the exhibition?"

"I have 200 paintings and I am only exhibiting 55 of them. Most of them are your favourite's dears."

"They are also fantastic it is tough to distinguish which one is the Best and which is the ideal love as you have such an artistic nature."

"You are so kind,"

Helen says, "You know this is going to be my first exhibition, but it is not going to be my last."

"Absolutely dear. It all depends on the sales as they say."

"Well, I sincerely hope that we managed to sell enough to cover the hire of the room and all the expenses."

"Honey, I believe it will work out perfectly as the advertising is extensive and we have personally invited many people. So therefore, I do believe it will be a success. Therefore, I do not think that you would have any reason to worry about any part of it. You will have also had plenty of replies to the invitations that you have sent out. Even one off the Mayor of Telford. Councillor Leon Murphy and his wife. They are definitely going to make an appearance honey."

"Yes, I know, dear but it is just pre-show nerves."

"I know I am right there with you. And you have the support of many other people." Helen says, "It is all quite exciting for me."

"It is also exciting for me too."

Charlie reaches out and put his hand on his wife's leg giving her a little comforting squeeze. Just to show that he is there for her. "Well I do think it is time for me to turn in as I do have an early start in the morning. I have a long drive into London,"

Helen says, "Will you be taking your motorbike."

"Yes, I definitely will. As it is the best thing to cut through the traffic. And it is also a lot cheaper on the parking :-)"

"Dear, it would be very nice if we went out for a nice ride out on the weekend, do you think so."

"Yes, that would be an excellent idea we can go and visit a few friends or we can just explore the countryside. How does that sound?"

"Perfect" Charlie takes another long sip from his wine glass emptying the glass.

Helen says, "You go to bed and I will be the mother and clear everything away as I can see that you are quite tired."

"Yes dear, I am absolutely shattered. Thank you."

Charlie stands up. Helen also stands up. They both give each other a very nice kiss good night.

Then Charlie walks off through the lounge up to their bedroom. Helen starts to clear up the glasses. Soon follows her husband up the stairs to the bedroom. As fellow walks into the bedroom, she noticed that Charlie is already in bed, settling down to go to sleep. Helen gets undressed out of the dressing gown and walks into the on suite.

She brushes her teeth and her hair, putting it into a ponytail not forgetting to moisturise before going to sleep after this. She walks back into the bedroom. To see her husband fast asleep. Then she climbs into bed. Charlie snuggles up to her and they both go to sleep.

CHAPTER 4

6:30 AM Charlie hovers his hand over the alarm clock, the alarm clock clicks. Just before the gongs and whistles go off. Charlie pushes the off button. In addition, takes a quick look at his wife who is fast asleep. She just seems so beautiful and relaxed with her eyes closed. Charlie leans forward and gently gives his wife a kiss on the cheek. Then gently proceeds to slowly pull his arm out from underneath his wife. Slowly, slowly does it. Making sure that he does not wake her. So thoughtful, as is. Another couple of inches and he will have his hand free. The pins and needles just start to take effect on his arm and hand. Charlie clenches his teeth to try to alleviate the tingling sensation in his dead, lifeless arm and gently pulls his fingers out from underneath his wife. She stirs slightly and rolls over to her right-hand side. Allowing Charlie to remove his hand totally.

He then sweeps his legs round off the bed and slips his slippers on. He can hear the birds tweeting as their early morning chorus and the stillness of the new morning.

Moving his arm and rolled it over the bed and starts moving his fingers, this just accentuates the pain of the pins and needles. It is just agonising. Soon the pain begins to subside and Charlie stood up and walked steadily into the on-suite bathroom scratching his sweaty nuts as he walks. He does the usual things that everybody else does in the morning. Then he brushes his teeth. A quick cold shower. To wake him up in the morning. Soon he is drying himself off taking extra special care of drying in between his toes. Foot preparation as they say.

Then walking straight back into the bedroom, he discovers that his wife had put his clothes out over the chair for him nicely fresh crisp ironed shirt. A glance over to the bed and through the early morning darkness you can discover his wife's figure through the shape of the bedclothes. While he is getting dressed.

Charlie looked over towards the alarm clock. 6:40 AM. He murmured to himself. "I must stimulate a move on." Charlie walked sleepily downstairs through the living room into the kitchen and proceeded to make himself a cup of coffee. Bacon and eggs, no perhaps a slice of toast. This typically takes only a few minutes. However, Charlie also had to get himself-ready for the motorcycle ride into London. While his coffee was cooling down slightly. In addition, his toast was about to pop. Charlie proceeded to pull on his leathers and a rucksack; this also held his jacket and his shoes in the rucksack. Everything that you would need for the doctor's surgery to look appropriate.

The toast is evenly browned and pops up quickly. Charlie quickly gets out an excellent piece of butter from the fridge and set forth to spread his toast. A quick bite of his toast and a swirl of dark brown and soon he is almost ready.

Into the garage, he goes carrying his coffee and a piece of toast stuffed in his mouth.

He looks over his blue and white motorbike BMW SPORTS 1000 RR, first, checking the chain tension with his foot and then checking the oil. A quick glimpse at the clutch reservoirs and he slid the key into the ignition. Shifting the key to the first placement and then the second. Watching the L.E.D screen and the cockpit of the motorcycle burst into life. As the rev counter needle swishes from 0 to 15,000 revs and back once more. "Everything seems fine in that respect." Only then, after everything is complete with all the checks, he pushes the starter button and turns the throttle.

Rolling the engine bursting into life. Charlie leaves it ticking over for a while. While he opens the electric garage doors. The early morning sun is just breaking the horizon it is only going to be a few minutes and the sun will be right up. To a beautiful sunrise. At that moment, something caught Charlie's eye. It was a young fox running briskly across the drive. Heading towards the fields. Charlie took out a moment and thought how incredible wildlife is in the morning. The Fox was quite startled from Charlie standing there. As the Fox looked and carried on running. In addition, as before as quick as he appeared he disappeared into the bushes. Charlie turned around and looked at his beautiful BMW RR 1000, purring like a kitten. So then, grabs hold of his helmet put it on nice and snuggly. Lifts his visor up.

The purring of the engine is slightly muffled over the snugly fitting ear plugs that Charlie was wearing.

Combined with the helmet everything goes into sports mode. The weather is beautiful it is at least 15° outside so the tarmac is at the perfect temperature. Charlie unplugs and pulls off the tyre warmers. And sits on his bike. Pulling his gloves on and giving a blip of the throttle. The choke on the engine automatically adjusts and the Engine of the motorcycle calms down. "She is warm now!" Charlie kicks the stand away and steps it into gear. In addition, slowly eases off the clutch and rolls the bike out of the garage. Charlie pushes a button on the motorbike handlebars. In addition, the garage doors begin to close.

Another blip of the throttle. He is off the clutch now is slow riding down his drive. A quick look left and a quick look right and then a quick life-saving manoeuvre. Charlie accelerates away from his drive. In addition, down the main road heading towards London. The power of the motorcycle is awesome and Charlie cannot wait to get it warmed up and is soon up to the speed limit within moments. The first bend his coming up to before the main roads an excellent right hand sweeping curve. The type of curve that you love to get your knee down on. However, not this morning as he likes to get oneself warmed up before piling on the power. Around this, bend nice and smooth with a little bit of a lean. A smooth gear changes the second third. Down the gears back into second. Lifesaving manoeuvre looking over the shoulder and indicating to turn onto the main highway. The satnav cries out His directions. In addition, he steadily turns on the power accelerating up through the gears. Charlie is listening to the engine as the high-power motorcycle revs a smooth tune and gear change from his super sports bike. Down the clear road in the early morning. Heading towards the first motorway junction on the M 54. The satnav calls out the directions once more. In addition, Charlie takes the turning onto the slip road onto the highway. Accelerating up the ramp towards the motorway junction you quickly look over his right shoulder to see that the way is clear; pulls onto the motorway accelerating and changing gear up to its cruising speed. The road was clear as a bell. He knows there are no speed cameras until just after the second bridge. Therefore, he pulls back the throttle and accelerate up to 130 miles an hour. Leaning down over the petrol tank behind the windshield of the bike. The bike smoothly stands up and becomes very responsive to any slight movement that Charlie commands to the motorcycle. Bridge 1 flies by bridge two flies by. Time to watch out for the speed cameras. Charlie knows that speed cameras will not catch anything over 150 miles an hour. Therefore, Charlie accelerates up to 165 mph and takes the C position on the road hugging the white line. Missing the road pressure sensors and flies down the road like a bullet. That is enough; furthermore, Charlie thinks. In addition, slows down to a gentle cruising speed of 100 miles an hour. At this rate, it will not take long to get into London. It is a lot faster than the train. Charlie sits up and rests his left hand on the top of his leg. Still the motorway roads are clear. As he is heading towards Cannock just as he is riding beneath the Shifnal (A41) Road junction to the motorway services, there are a couple of cars joining the highway. And one other motorcycle. Charlie pulls out into the overtaking lane and lets the traffic joining the motorway. With a nod to the other motorcyclist response with a nod, back. Four minutes later, Charlie is closer, is about to pass the Cannock off ramp motorway junction slip road, and will soon be joining the M6. Slowing down for the nice long bends around on to the junction as both motorcyclists join up on the motorway. Charlie points at his helmet. This is a signal for the other motorcyclist to join in his bike-to-bike Bluetooth radio. The rider puts his thumb up to acknowledge. Click, click, crackle, and crackle. The speakers make the noise as the helmets are pairing up. The noise in Charlie's helmet. "Testing, testing 1.2.3 can you hear me, Charlie?" "Yes clear as a bell, I can hear you clearly Magnum, good morning." "Hello Charlie, it is a fine day for a ride." "Yes, Magnum than I thought I would take my bike to work today, you must have had the same idea as I."

"Yes!"

Charlie says, "Magnum what is your 20 today?"

"Birmingham. But I will be finished for 4:30 today."

The two motorcycles slip through the traffic with these, as they are looking out for each other being each other's eyes. It is important to keep safe on the motorway as one little incident means death.

"Magnum, you have a cager who is a bit of an idiot. He is not giving you any room. So accelerate."

"Thanks, Charlie" as Magnum exonerates to get away from this cager danger the rule of thumb, keep as much distance away from any vehicle as possible especially at high speed on the motorway. Magnum manages to survive this one, but it was close. A couple more miles down the road and soon the traffic starts to build up especially around the M5 junction. Therefore, Magnum and I begin to filter through the traffic. Soon we are passed the junction M5. The road clears up around the long bend over the motorway bridge.

Magnum guns it. In addition, he gets his knee down around the bend. It is a remarkable sight. To see a skilled rider taking a long curve at high speed. Charlie follows him in the slipstream of Magnum's motorcycle they are both down hugging the tank at speeds in excess of 74 miles an hour more like 120. To be precise. There is nothing like the freedom of the roads.

Soon it is time for Magnum to leave the motorway and heading into Birmingham. Magnum raised his left hand to salute Charlie and thanked him for the ride. Charlie returns his salute. In addition, a few last words were spoken. "Thanks, bro," Charlie says, "You are a welcome bro."

Charlie carries on riding down the M6 towards his destination in London. 155 miles in total in a car would take approximately 3 hours 30 minutes via the M40. However, Charlie manages to do it in 2 hours 10 minutes the average of 90 miles an hour. Soon Charlie joins up with the M40 and is cruising through the traffic with ease. There remain absolutely no problems or issues with the rest of the ride as he is cruising down the motorway. The only problem is the sunrise is in your eyes. Which makes it difficult occasionally? So therefore, he has to adjust the speed to suit the road conditions.

A few nice fast sports cars want to have a play. In addition, try to compete with the voracious power of this BMW RR. 1000 (2 Back page links to a video) as you can see, the bike is king of the hill.

20 minutes later Charlie is heading to the London central. The traffic is not unusually heavy in town today, but you still have to look out for the idiots. Definitely, think for them

as well as yourself. The only way is to ride safe. Pass the Ladbrokes hotel on the BBC radio and television studios and soon Charlie is on the final approach to his medical practice.

As he turns up, you can see the queue outside the doors stretching down the street. It is agreeing to be another one of those busy days looking at the size of the line.

The telephone rings and he answers it by pushing a button on his helmet.

"Hello, darling."

Charlie's wife asks. "Have you arrived safely?"

"Not enough time honey, just parking up."

"Did you sleep well?"

"Yes, I did, it was a lovely evening with you last night."

"Thank you, honey."

Charlie goes on to say. "Are you making your final arrangements today for your exhibition?"

"Yes, I am doing that exactly."

"Okay, honey well, I love you loads and you have a nice day take care and whenever there is anything that I can do to help you give me a call xx."

"Thank you, darling, I will see you this evening when you get home. Xx"

Charlie put the phone down, pulls his motorcycle into the car park at the back of the medical practice.

In addition, walked in through the back door into the main foyer of the practice.

"Any messages for me," He asks his delightful receptionist.

She says, "no messages today Dr"

"Thank you, Can you make me a nice coffee please and bring it through into my office. I will need a nice coffee before I start my practice."

Charlie walked into his office closes the door behind himself. Then walked across the room, and walked through another doorway. In this room, there is just one single couch, and a wardrobe full of his motorcycle gear of where he is changed.

Charlie hears a knock at the door!

"Hello."

"Hello, Dr here is your coffee."

"Just put it there on a desk please, and send in the first curly toes customer."

Curly toes are medical slang for people who do not look after themselves you know just like the down and outs. As they do not bother cutting their toenails.

"Yes, Dr"

Charlie finishes getting himself ready and walks out of the small annex room closing the private annex door behind him. And sits down behind his desk. Reaching forward and moving his lamp slightly to the left. Then picking up his coffee. Turning the computer on and setting up for his first patient of the day.

Then he takes a nice long sip of his coffee.

And a rock back in his leather chair and stretches his arms in the air just making oneself comfortable as it seems like it is going to be one of those days.

A few minutes pass's and his computer come is up online. Therefore, he pushes the intercom button to call in his first patient of the day.

A quick read the familiar patient's notes.

The patient walks in limping.

Charlie thinks to himself, keeping a serious expression. "What sort of bullshit! Is this guy going to come out with today?"

"Take a seat." so, the patient struggles to walk across the room towards the chair.

The smell of cigarette smoke and a bad smell of beer in the air envelop the room. Making the doctor Choke slightly.

Finally, the patient struggles to sit down, making all sorts of noises of pain and discomfort.

Charlie asks, "What seems to be the problem and how can I help you."

The man moans and grumbles, as it is obvious he is intoxicated.

"It is my ankle it hurts a lot."

"Okay then let us have a look at it can you take your shoes and socks off, please."

The young man takes his shoes and socks off with a little bit of a struggle but still manages to do it. At this moment, I was still watching him making sure that everything else was okay with him. In other words, he is back. A quick visual diagnosis and there is no problems with him I am sure. At least with his back.

By this time, the room soon starts to smell of the pungent smelly sweaty socks and BO.

The person's feet look rather dirty and a bad case of athlete's foot, so I decided to put some rubber gloves on too-be safe. I knelt down in front of him. Then started to examine the opposite foot that he was limping on. Just to catch him out a little bit. "Yes this looks rather bad you have quite a bit of bruising there, does this hurt" as Charlie pushed his finger into the joint of his ankle. The drunken man moved in his seat grabbing the armchair as if he was showing pain. Charlie looked over at the other ankle and could not see any difference. And then sat back up in his chair. "What can one do to help you then?" the Dr asked.

"I would like some painkillers, please."

Charlie taps away on his computer and prints out a prescription for him.

Then hands the order over to the alcoholic man, of whom he smiled and slurred, "Thank you Dr you are a Gordon." The patient then stood up and started limping out of the door on the wrong leg. The leg that he went in on was perfect and now the good leg was bad. This is obviously the case that he was after painkillers to sell on the open market or just to take for his own personal enjoyment. The door closed. Charlie immediately sprayed air freshener, changed his gloves, and then wrote up a little report about the young man. About his substance abuse also the prescription of vitamins, that he had just been prescribed to this curly toes person.

Then takes another long sip from his coffee cup. Charlie then presses the intercom button and calls in his next patient.

The door opens.

A young girl walks in; to look at her with a first glance you would not say there is anything wrong with her.

"Please take a seat."

The young girl walks over and takes a seat next to the desk.

"Now what seems to be the problem with you, my dear?"

The young girl seemed quite embarrassed. At first glance.

"Will Dr I do not really know what it is, but I have lumps under my arm and in my mouth, I also have a large rash on my belly."

The doctor looked down at his records. You cannot see that she has been visiting this practice very much. In fact, it would say this would be the first ever meeting with the doctor.

So taking a sympathetic course.

"Do you mind if I examine you and have a look at the problem."

"Not at all Dr!"

"Can you get onto the couch, lift your top up please, and show me your rash."

Patient walks over to the other end of the room, gets onto the couch, and lifts up her top to show the rash.

Charlie immediately realised what this could be. As he had seen it so many times before. Never before on such a young girl sadly though.

"Can you lay down please thank you?"

The young girl lies down on the couch. She is a quite petite and beautiful thing she is.

Charlie puts on some new gloves and starts to examine her belly. And finds that there are lumps underneath the skin. In addition, the rash looks quite aggressive red and black rash does not disappear after the pressure is applied to it. The doctor looks up at her neck. In addition, realises that she has a small fading love bite on the neck. This looks like a high-five to me he thinks.

The girl's stomach muscles jump a little bit from the pain. As her belly was pressed.

"Does that hurt?"

"Yes, a little bit Dr just a small bit."

"Okay that will conclude the examination, you may get off the couch and get yourself dressed."

Young girl gets off the couch gets herself dressed and walks over to where she was sitting before. Her skin had a slightly greasy look about it and she had occasional spots on her face as well as a rash. Things do not seem too good for this girl.

"I am going to send you for some blood tests at the Telford Hospital."

Charlie types a little note up on the computer and then printed off.

He hands the note to the young girl along with a sick note for her work.

The girl looks around to Charlie, the doctor. And asks "is this just the flu or is it more serious?"

Charlie did not want to worry the girl even though he thought that it could quite possibly be HIV.

"We will see after the blood tests."

The girl smiles and the worried look dissipate from her face, showing a beautiful, pleasing smile.

"Take care now and come back when you have had your blood test it should take about a week." The girl picks up the papers that her doctor had given her. In addition, she says, "Thank you Dr" And then the young girl stood up and walked out of the room. Charlie starts typing up his report. As he does, believe that this girl has HIV. (Suspicion of HIV.)

Well, that is pretty much how the day goes on, patient after patient and the day slips by.

It is now approximately 1:45 PM and Charlie is preparing to finish up at the practice a bit more early today and head home. As it is, Friday! The practice will be closing at 4:00 pm. In addition, it is his wife's big evening at her art exhibition exhibiting all of her fabulous paintings.

He gives his Wife a call from the office. "Hello honey, is it convenient to talk?"

"Oh yes my darling yes it is, is everything alright."

"Yes everything's fine here, I was just letting you know that I am heading home."

"That is wonderful dear looking forward to seeing you."

"And I am looking forward to seeing you as well. Is everything running smoothly for this evening?"

"Everything is perfect. And thank you for the lovely flowers by Interflora you are a big softy."

"What flowers, :-)"

"There is only one person in my life that remembers my favourite flowers and you are the one, so do not pull my leg dear."

"Oh yes, I remember now."

"What do you mean I remember now is it that you have just got your secretary to send them out to me."

"Absolutely not dear I organised and phoned the florist up myself. I was only joking."

"See darling I know you so well."

"Okay honey love you loads must speak to you later as I am about to get ready to beat the Friday traffic."

"Okay dear, I love you too make sure you ride safely on that bike."

"I always do honey."

"See you soon then."

A voice in the background calls out, "Helen, where would you like this one hung."

"Better go now dear I am very busy."

"By-by."

Charlie puts the telephone down.

He begins to take his jacket off and walks into the back room to be changed.

This only takes a few minutes for him to change into his motorbike gear and then walks out of his office with his helmet under his arm.

Charlie walks close by to the receptionist and says, "Have a good weekend, and I will see you on Monday."

"You to Dr, you have a good weekend, I hope that everything goes well at the wife's presentation of her art exhibition. The girls in the back office will be there. However, I am afraid that I cannot make it. Please send your good wife Helen my apologies."

"That is okay dear I understand."

Charlie smiles and walks away and through the back door leading into the small private car park at the rear.

There it is, still there, his beautiful BMW S 1000 CC RR. Charlie gives the bike a quick once over, first check the lights and then the oil levels through the little window on the side of the engine. He slides the key into the ignition and pulls his helmet on at the same time glancing at the brake fluid level on the handlebars of the motorbike. He mounts his motorcycle like a fine stallion.

Press the button to start the engine a quick look around over both shoulders just to be safe. Charlie then pulls away out of the car park and onto the main road with a life-saving glance. Charlie can see the traffic is not too bad in the middle of the afternoon. Even though the cars were near bumper-to-bumper. However, they have left a nice little route on the left-hand side just wide enough for the motorcycle to get through with ease. Therefore, Charlie takes this route. Charlie thinks it would be nice with a bit of music and he starts the music by pushing a button on his helmet and he says, "Play all songs." Soon the music floods into his helmet the sounds of the Opera. There is nothing wrong with a bit of Beethoven while driving through London. It drowns out the honking of horns. Busy, noisy, revving engines. However, not so loud, so he cannot hear anything. Smoothly he drives through the traffic making his way towards the M40 motorway. Just two sets of red traffic lights and he is soon out of London. He thinks about his wife on her maiden voyage of her first art exhibition. It helps him pass the time of day and gives him some great comfort knowing that his wife is doing something that she loves.

The satnav comes up with a warning that the traffic is obstructed on the island slip road North and southbound on the M 40. The satnav automatically takes an alternative route. Turning the music down, within his helmet and read directing Charlie to the next junction on the M 40. It is another 25 miles away. This slows Charlie down, putting an extra 20 minutes on his journey. Blasted he thinks. Anyway, it cannot be availed. Before Charlie knows it, he is cutting through some rather derelict rough housing estates. Just to dilute as much time off this diversion principal as possible. He Notices children running in the streets with no shoes on in their bare feet. He cannot believe his eyes. Children so close to London or in our country cannot afford the necessities of shoes on their feet. He had definitely stumbled over a poverty-stricken region. Charlie mine started working overtime how could he help them. He knows that handing out thousands of pounds to these people will not make any difference. So there must be some kind of a way to help these people. Education that is its pedagogy. Could he donate some money to the local school to help the schools to help the children? As this is, the most important matter is education. If the children were educated and maybe the parents will follow suit. Then the whole thing will change for the future. He knows that there is no fast fix in anything like this poverty on our streets. However, knowing that there must be some way we can facilitate.

Thank God, there is the signboard for the M40 motorway. At that moment, a tennis ball bounces along the footpath and then onto the road. Charlie immediately applies his brakes. In addition, slows down to around 5 mph. Then with no hesitation or without warning a young boy raced out of his garden gate straight across a footpath and right in front of Charlie's motorcycle. Charlie was already geared up for this incident and had already stopped. A young boy was shocked, as he did not consider the vehicle or even Charlie. As he had already stepped in front of the motorbike on the road. No kidding you, this young boy would have been dead!

Did I already say that? No way would this small fry would have survived a motorcycle impact at 30 miles an hour. That would not have been good for any of us. Nevertheless, the boy smiled and grabbed hold of his tennis ball and proceeded to run back across the road, through the gate, and into his garden. How fast your life can change in an illustration instance.

Charlie slowly pulls away and drove off the housing estate. Within moments, he was turning left onto the on-ramp of the M40 motorway, steady acceleration up to 75 miles an hour up the on-ramp and onto the busy motorway. The music changes on his selection, the Eye of the Tiger begins to beat. The boxing, Rocky song. Charlie has a good notion of his body and he just wants to ride. Riding like the eye of the Tiger. Cutting through traffic. Like a blade. The BMW RR 1000 is perfect for this sort of task on the motorway. Charlie takes it steady all the way home up to the M54 motorway. He gives his wife a quick call as he normally does when he is approaching the M54 motorway. Just a drop call. The phone only rings twice just to let his wife knows that he is on his way home and he is safe.

15 minutes later, Charlie is pulling up to his drive at the household. Everything seems fine as he approaches so he pushes the button for the garage's door the garage roles opens quickly. Moreover, Charlie rolls his motorcycle into the garage and parks up. Another click of the button and the garage door closes.

His wife should be heading home soon to get changed into fresh clothes ready for the late afternoon exhibition. The art exhibition will proceed on into the late evening. As we plan to create a little bit of a celebration of it.

Charlie walks out of the garage and into the house and runs upstairs to get his selfish shower. "I have got to get myself out of these clothes," and soon Charlie was in the shower. A quick wash and the job are done. Time to decompress for a few moments with a beautiful cup of coffee in the living room. Charlie wanders downstairs through the living room and into the kitchen to make oneself coffee with just a towel wrapped around his waist.

He likes this free feeling to be able to walk around one's own home in a towel, is one of the life's little luxuries. Charlie is making himself comfortable with an excellent cup of coffee in the living room. Knowing that he only has 30 minutes or so before his wife turns up. Charlie catches up with the news in the local newspaper. The art exhibition advertised for this evening, his wife's art exhibition. Charlie studies the text of the article quite thoroughly. While relaxing over a hot cup of coffee.

Charlie soon dozed off in his easy chair; he thought it was only for a minute or two. Nevertheless, his wife awaked him.

"A busy day honey. " Charlie stretches in his chair and yawns. He blinks a couple of times at his wife.

Moreover, he says sleepily, "I am sorry I must have dozed off for a moment Have you seen the Publishing the article in a newspaper."

"Yes, honey I have! I think I have done a splendid job of the advert."

"What time is it, dear?"

"Well, honey, you need to get dressed as soon as possible, as we have approximately 15 minutes before we leave."

"Yes dear, I will get a move on right now! But by the way, you look absolutely fabulous."

Charlie's wife spins around a ballet pirouette showing off her new clothes with a loving smile.

"Do you really think so honey? You do not believe that it is too much or too little do you."

"My love you look like an angel and artist Angel."

"So is this too much then is it do you think I need to tuck the wings in a little bit :-)."

"You were just funny now are you not?"

"When I say you are an angel it is because you are one especially in my eyes."

Charlie eases himself out of the chair and makes haste to get you ready. Charlie disappears up the stairs and leaves his wife behind in the living room. Helen's telephone rings. "Hello, Helen here, how can I help?" A man speaks with a broad Australian accent. "I have seen the advert in the newspaper for the exhibition I would be interested in a piece in my house. Did you do any large canvases for in your art exhibition?" " Yes I did so sir, what sort of work would you be looking for." " Well, I need something rather large to cover a large wall." " Well, I have a fantastic waterfall that I have only finished last year that is my centrepiece of the entire collection. As the Blue Lagoon has inspired me in Italy when I spent a short holiday break over there. But it's hard to express all this over the phone so we will look forward to seeing you at the exhibition, then we can carry on with this conversation then looking forward to meeting you." " Yes I agree well I shall be round there about 8:30 PM. Thank you for your time and will see you soon." " Thank you, see you soon and goodbye." " Till then-then, goodbye."

Charlie walks down the stairs straight back into the living room, dressed crisp white shirt and black jacket the suit to match very smartly.

Helen says, "Something is missing here."

Charlie replies "Oh yes."

Charlie puts both of these arms out in front of him. It is not possible to see anything on his wrists as his wife was expecting a beautiful golden Rolex watch.

Charlie smiles and claps his hands at the same time saying, "Abracadabra." As if by magic his Rolex appears. His new Rolex watch slides down under his shirt from the top of his arm onto his wrist and Charlie just flamboyantly lifted his arm up and closed the clasps. With a little tug on each one of his cuffs of his shirt. With a sparkle from each one of his diamond cufflinks.

His wife smiles on amazement and says, "beautiful."

"I would never have forgotten to put this on I have been thinking about Wearing it all day." Her eyes light up and she smiles.

Writes: Dear let us get going because we are running short on time.

Husband and wife walk briskly to the car and drive to the exhibition together.

CHAPTER 5

Arriving at the exhibition. "Please tell me your first impressions dear." Charlie turns around and looked at his wife, and says, "I will honey, and you can definitely count on me to do this for you."

Has the celebrity's spiritual woman arrived? What was her name again?" Helen says, "you need to say that you have forgotten her name already?" Charlie says, "Yes dear I have. It has just slipped my mind. Can you just remind me, please?" Helen says, "Just remember this. Lesley Fozzard, Lesley Fozzard, Lesley Fozzard, She is a particular friend to me, and she has been great inspiration for my artwork. Lesley Fozzard is an amazing person with the calming nature of the angels. Come on in, honey let's get into the exhibition." Charlie unbuckled his seatbelt and puts his hand out to touch his wife's leg. She turns around sweetly as Charlie gives her a supportive kiss with a touch of romance to show his support. Helen responds by touching Charlie's face with her soft, gentle hand. They both then disembark from the car and take a steady walk hand-in-hand towards the exhibition. The click of her stiletto heels and the occasional car hooting in the distance complimented a quiet relaxing dusk. It is a pleasant feeling of the crisp evening. As they, both tiptoe up the stairs towards the exhibition door.

Charlie, leans forward and grabbed hold of the door handle and opened the large door, holding it open for his wife to walk through. They both walked. The smell of the oil paintings is strong. The first thing that Charlie notices. While they are both walking into the exhibition Fourier. Helen and I were greeted by the proprietor of the Establishment and introduced himself To Charlie. As Carl Manson. "Hello Charlie it is my pleasure to meet you my name is Carl Manson. I am the proprietor. If there is anything that one will do to assist you and your good lady wife Helen, please do not hesitate to ask." Charlie says, "It is my pleasure to meet you, Carl." While shaking his hand with a sturdy grip. Carl then says, "Would you like a glass of champagne?" Charlie and Helen accepted with a small nod. A young man walked over carrying a silver tray with two fluted crystal long stemmed champagne glasses upon it. This was a nice feeling as we were welcomed by the owner of the establishment given us the hospitality of the greetings that we would be expecting for our guests also to receive.

The Champagne bubbles tickle Charlie's nose as he was sipping out of the glass. Charlie looked around the room and could see that it was not just clean room, but there were many little other rooms off the main hall.

Through the lobby, there was a small stage with the biggest painting that his wife had ever painted up on the stage mounted on the wall. Carl walked Helen and Charlie, into the main hall to show Charlie, the exhibition. Charlie says, "You have picked just the perfect place to show your art my darling." "My dear Charlie you are so sweet." As Helen, smiles at her husband holding the long fluted champagne glass in her delicate fingers. Carl Manson says, "I shall leave you to get on with things I will be about, just raise your hand or give me a call and I will come over to assist you." Helen says, "Thank you, Carl, you are an excellent support." Charlie also adds, "it is a pleasure to meet you, Carl," and Charlie gives Carl a little nod out of respect for his service. Carl, the proprietor, then walks away. Leaving Helen and Charlie together in the middle of the room. Charlie looks around the room and spins on his heel slowly as he does it, taking in the pleasant delights of the visual arts that his wife had painted and worked on for so many years. The feeling of enlightenment comes after Charlie and he expresses his joy to his wife. By saying, "I have never seen your work so delightfully displayed in such a professional manner before. " Charlie walks over to a large painting, he reminisces at the time when this painting was done. "This picture brings back memories of when we first met. Does it not, my dear," she says. "Yes, love, this was the day when you turned up on your motorcycle and left it parked up outside my house." a rendition of a traditional Norton motorcycle. "Honey, you have captured this remarkably well. The depth of field just makes me want to lean forward and touch it. This brings that beautiful day flooding back to me Darling. "Helen smiles. Charlie raises his champagne glass to his wife and salutes the artist in respect of a job well done. And clinked his glass with his wife" to the success." They both said together "I will drink to that." Charlie started to feel himself fill-up with tears of tender emotions. Helen noticed this. And said, "These are the first days that have been immortalised in the memories of our relationship of the first moments when I actually fell in love with you. Charlie leaned forward and gave his wife a kiss and a hug, his wife responded romantically and put her arms around him. They were both standing in the middle of the exhibition all alone in such a romantic setting that in itself could be the beginning of a beautiful love story.

Helen says we must get ready, "as we will be meeting the first guests very soon."

Helen and Charlie separate from their embrace. Helen says, "I have something to do to get prepared for the speech when people arrive, so please darling, take your time and have a look at the paintings. " Helen then walks over towards Carl. In addition, Carl helps her up onto the stage. In addition, start showing Helen something on the tablet computer. Charlie automatically thinks that it is something to do with the presentation of the centrepiece within the art exhibition. Therefore, Charlie leaves them to it and walks around the exhibition looking at the paintings. Bringing back memories of his past relationship with his wife. Opening up memories that have been long forgotten. He came across a picture that was painted on the balcony in a villa in Spain. This painting captured the hot sunny days. In addition, he could actually feel the warmth emanating from the picture as if it was a 3-D photograph. Every single work of art that he looked at had a calming appeal to it. The colours and brush strokes would fit any household environment. With a modern twist. Charlie, felt that he could step into each painting as they unlocked beautiful memories as he is looking at them as he wandered dreamily around the rooms as he is reminiscing to himself about his wife and years gone by.

Time slipped away and the first guests started to appear, like Charlie, was in one of the rooms admiring the beautiful art, off from the main hall. Charlie could see and hear the noise of new people turning up also the expressions of pleasure that they were presenting to each other as they entered the art exhibition. So then, Charlie walked around to the main door to meet his wife, greeting the new clients that were coming in through the door one after the other. Every one of them wanted to envision the artist. Charlie stood back from the spotlight and let his wife meet and greet each person as they came in through the door after collecting a fluted bubbly champagne glass. Soon the room was filled with people talking about the paintings. Everybody was dressed in their finest. The waiters walked around with silver trays and canapés. We serve the public interest! The delight of witnessing his wife smile was a pleasant feeling to Charlie. Soon it was time for the speech, Carl Manson, introduced the artist by tapping a glass to bring the Attention to Everybody That the Speech was about to Be Presented by the Artist Helen Summers.

"Ladies and gentlemen, I would like to present the artist Helen Summers. It Gives Me Great Pleasure To Present the Artist Helen Summers. So Please Ladies and Gentlemen Can You Put Your Hands Together for Helen Summers." The Applause Rang out As Everybody in the Room Applause. Charlie Thought to Himself She Has used Her Maiden Name Not Her Married Name. This Hurt on Slightly But He Understood As She Started Painting Long before She Met Charlie And That Is How She Signed Her Paintings.

Helen Stood On the Stage Looking Out To Everybody That Was Given Helen the Centre of Attention There Must Have Been a full house approximately 150 People Which Is a Large Gathering for this Art Exhibition. To See over 1000 Paintings.

"Hello, Ladies and Gentlemen. It gives me great pleasure to open my first art exhibition.

First, I would like to say Thank You! Very Much for Coming to My Accredited Fine Art Exhibition of My Personal Art The First Exhibition of Its Kind That I Have Presented To the Public. Please Feel Free to Mingle around the Paintings and speak to me or my assistants And Have a Chat about Any Artwork That Takes Your Interest, as I will be grateful to assist you.

I Started Painting When I Was a Young Girl. With Watercolours. However, I Only Started Using acrylic and oils When I First Met My Husband. The First Oil Painting That I Have Ever Done Is the Motorcycle, The Norton Motorcycles That You Can See Behind You. "Helen Points in the Direction of the Painting. Nearly everybody in the Audience Turned around to look at the Painting that Carl Manson was standing by and pointing out The Work of Art. At That Moment, Charlie Noticed A Tall Gentleman Staring At His Wife But Not Taking Any Notice of the Painting. He Was the Tallest Person in the Room I Should Say. He is standing Very Still and upright. As He Was Looking Directly at Charlie's Wife. Charlie could see that there was some kind of connection there For a Moment.

Helen Started to Speak Once Again. "And This Painting Here Which Is My Centrepiece." Pointing up to a Large Canvas behind the Stage "Is My Final Workings of the Exhibition Up to Date. As You Can See, the Water Flows down the Waterfall into the Blue Lagoon. There Was Something Magical about This Place That I Could Not Share in One-Dimensional. So I Have Decided to Painting Two-Dimensional Is of Light, The First I Mention of Light Is

What You Can See Now. In addition, the Second I Mention of Light Is What I am about to Show You. "You Could Feel the Tension of the Audience Gasp in Amazement. As They Are about to See Something That Has Never Been Presented in a Painting before. Helen Says, "But First of All, I Would like to Present A Spiritual Friend To Cleanse The Paintings And the Audience So That You Can See The Amazing Differences in Light That an Artist Can See In the Best Way That I Can Present to You. Can You Please Show Your Appreciation to Lesley Fozzard? Another Round of Applause Rings out As Lesley Fozzard Walks Gracefully onto the Stage. "Hello, Ladies and Gentlemen. You Are Probably Wondering What I Have in My Hand. It Is an Ancient Thing That Our Ancestors Used to Use To Cleanse The Good Spirits. "Lesley Fozzard Was Holding in Her Hand a Sensual Candle of a collection of herbs That Brought a Beautiful Fragrance into the Room. The Smoke Wafted through the Audience and As the Smoke Touched Your Skin. It Seemed to Do Something by Collecting The Bad Feelings from Your Body. In addition, Carry them away and out through the Ventilation System. "Please Allow the Smoke to Carry and Take Away Anything That You That Should Not Be within the Room. " You Could Feel a Sense Of A delightful magical Feeling That Was All Good inside as the Smoke and the magic herbs did Their Work. This brought a wonderful happy Feeling through the Audience. It Was a Twist Of the Old and the New Coming Together For the Future Of Good Things And Protection Of the Audience. Then Lesley Fozzard Walked off the Stage and proceeded to walk among The Audience. However, There Was One Man. That Was Desperately Trying to Avoid the Smoke As Lesley Walked around the Room. In addition, this was the Tall Gentleman That Was Staring at Charlie's

Wife only Moments before. Lesley Then Said a Closing Prayer And Walked Out Of the Main Door And Let the Smoke Wafted Out Of the Door. You Can See the Smiles on People's Faces Lighten up. Everybody's Good Energies Just Seem to Come to the Surface. Charlie Thought to Himself, Whatever It Was That Was in Those Herbs and Spices They Seem to Have Done the Trick as Charlie could feel the Goosebumps on his skin and the prickly sensation running down the back of his neck. Helen then Says, "It Is Now Time to Show You the Other Dimensional of My Painting. Can We Have the Lights Dimmed Please?"

The Lights Dimmed Down. In addition, an Amazing Sight Came over Everyone in the Room as the Painting seemed to Move Slightly as a Waterfall shimmered through the subtle hazy smoke As the Lights Grew Darker. However, the Light from the Painting Still Stayed the same and seemed to assist the cleansing of the room. A Fluorescent Bluey Green Glow came from the Painting As the main Lights Turned off. The Relaxing, Calming Herbs from Lesley Fozzard happened to be working their Magic Along with the Amazing Waterfall Feature oil painting That Was Glowing in the Dark in amazement In Front of Everyone's Eyes. Carl Manson turned on the surround sound stereo system, flooding the exhibition with music playing a soothing sound of the actual waterfall that Helen Painted as the lights dim. Oh, it is all just so delightful! Helen proceeded to explain, "I Have founded An Amazing Pigment That I Am Going to Keep Secret That I Am Using in My Paintings to Present This Glorious Effect to you. At What You Can See in Front of You. Astonishingly the audience as they stood there with their mouths open to the remarkable cleansing beauty of the waterfall

"I will leave you for a Moment to take in the beauty of the Painting and to absorb the Tranquil Movements of the Waterfall."

A Silence of Amazement came over the Audience as They All Watched the Painting in the Darkroom Come to Life right before their very eyes.

Two minutes later Helen asked Carl quietly, "Carl You Can Raise the Lights Now." As the Lights Raised Everybody Applauded Helen Summers For Her Fantastic Amazing Work. The Applause Seemed to Last and Last. Helen smiles A Beautiful Smile to Receive the Incredible Display of Gratitude from the Audience for Her Works of Art. The Painting Seem to Changed Again, and Returned Back to Its Original Form Of a spectacular Waterfall.

And the Applause Rang out. "I Now Present This Art Exhibition Well and Truly Open." Another Applause rang out. Helen Walked down off the Stage and Started to Mingle with Her Audience. The Tall Gentleman in the Audience Just Seems to Be Transfixed By the Waterfall Painting on the Stage. He Stood There Are Still in the Crowd As Everybody Was Walking around He Was Still Stood Staring at the Painting. Helen Walked towards Charlie as People in the Audience Were Congratulating Her on Her Work and the Presentation of the Exhibition. Charlie Could Hear All Sorts of Words of Encouragement To His Wife. As Helen Walks through and Approaches Charlie. The Gentleman That Was Staring at the Painting Walks over to Charlie's Wife. In addition, with a Smile He Introduces Himself. And Starts Talking about the Painting. Helen Stood There for A Few Moments and Listen to What He Had to Say. Then this Man Leaned forward and kissed her on the Cheek. In addition, began shaking Her Hand as if they had merely completed a business transaction. Helen, Then Raised Her Hand and Carl Manson, Came over And Started Talking to the Gentleman. Helen, then soon Walked Over to Charlie. And Said, "So What Did You Think about My Speech than Honey." "Amazingly My Love I Never Knew that You Had Such a Pleasant Powerful Energy of Public Speaking."

Charlie and Helen Started Talking to a Few of Their Friends That Have Been Invited To the Social Occasion of the Opening of Her Exhibition. Charlie Looked over, Notice That the Gentleman the Tall Gentleman Had Disappeared, and Carl Manson. Charlie Said, "Did You Notice the Tall Gentleman. Yes, I answered. He Has Just Bought the Large Painting. "Charlie Showed His Appreciation by Saying How Wonderful my Dear. " A Waiter Appears with Another Tray of Canapés. Charlie Helps Is Self to a Salmon and Cream Cheese Canapé and bikes it in half.

The exhibition rooms were all quite crowded, as many people were admiring the art around the chambers. "Hello Dr" a well-dressed man appeared from the crowd with a young woman on his arm. He said, "It is a pleasant surprise seeing you here doctor." Charlie replied, "thank you." As Charlie was just clear in his mouth from the delicious canapé. Charlie puts out his hand to shake the man's hands that he cannot recognise now. Charlie understands that the man remembers him quite well from somewhere. However, Charlie cannot recall or recognise him. However, Charlie makes polite conversation as if they were friends for years or associates. So Charlie says, "what do you think of the exhibition?" "Well, Dr my new fiancée and I were admiring the artist's incredible depth of detail and remarking on how well travelled she must be. My fiancée and I were primarily interested in the Norton motorcycle artistic piece."

Charlie says, "Yes the Norton motorcycle is quite an impressive composition. " The man's fiancée says, "Craig really loves the Norton motorcycles as he bears quite a collection in the garage, Craig thought that it would be very nice to have an oil painting in his office. So I think I am going to treat him to one for his birthday. "Charlie says, "what an excellent gift, which is it the ones that you prefer Craig." Craig replies, "the Norton motorcycle that Helen was talking about the time she fell in love with her husband. As I know that this painting has been produced out of love, so it seems to emanate out of the picture interpretative into the laws of motorcycles. So this is the one for me, I do believe. "Charlie ""I sincerely think that you have a perfect choice. But you will have to move fast as I understand that these paintings are selling like hotcakes." Craig says, "yes they are and I have already reserved this actual oil painting here. "A waiter walks by with flutes of champagne on a tray. Craig's fiancée leans forward and helps herself to a flute of bubbly champagne and Craig and Charlie. As they make small talk over their champagne surrounded by fabulous art and a collection of fascinating people. All three of them talk about art and business. Charlie could see that his wife was very busy. As Carl Manson was busy writing down names and addresses and taking payments for the paintings. Each picture was marked sold by a little red sticky backed paper circle, placed beside of the description of the composition description on the wall. Charlie says to Craig, "so your passion is Norton motorcycles?" "Yes they are and it is also my career as I rebuild old vintage bikes. In addition, I always prefer to work on the Norton's. "Charlie nods in appreciation. Then Charlie says, "Please excuse me as I need to look at a few more paintings." It is nice to meet you once again Doctor. In addition, shakes Charlie's hand. "It is my pleasure and then Charlie politely withdraws from the couple. For some reason, Charlie just felt a little bit uncomfortable. In the company of these, two people whom he did not recognise. Even though they seem to know him so well. Charlie made his way to the other side of the room and met up with a few of his colleagues from his practice. There he felt a lot better in his own environment. His wife glanced over at Charlie and smile. And Charlie mouths the words across the room." Everything is going well." Helen replied with a nod and a smile. In addition, replied by mouthing the words back to her husband silently. "I love you honey" and blows Charlie a kiss. Charlie responded by catching the kiss in mid-air on his hand and plucking it from the air and placing it on his lips. And then carried on talking and socialising with his colleagues.

"Hello! Charlie, come and join us, we were just talking about The Celebrity Lesley Fozzard. Is not she just wonderful. "Charlie replies to his colleague." Lesley Fozzard is an amazing woman and she has an amazing skill and quality that brings peace and serenity everywhere she goes. As we have all felt this evening." We can well understand why she is the chosen by the celebrities on the television as she has a special gift that brings a calming nature to everyone that she meets. And touches with her smoke." Charlie says, "did you manage to see the gentleman standing in the middle of the audience when Lesley Fozzard came onto the stage?" Charlie's colleague says, "Yes I did how bizarre he just tried to avoid the smoke. But the smoke enveloped the room and it was not possible for him to escape totally." Charlie says, "I wonder what it means?" His colleague says, "I have no idea, maybe he just does not like smoke or maybe he was a different foreign people have different religions these days." Charlie says, "yes I know, so many different religions so many different faiths. Or maybe he is just afraid of the smoke for some reason?" The colleague, says, "I really do not have any idea of this, but it is worrying as he was acting quite unusual."

"Here comes your wife Charlie," as Charlie turns around to see his wife approaching with the celebrity Lesley Fozzard. "Hello, darling." Charlie put his hand out to guide his wife into the circle of friends. Instantly the feeling of Lesley Fozzard in the circle made an incredible impression on the people that I cannot explain. "Hello Miss Fozzard," Lesley said, "now please do not worry about the formalities please call me Lesley." Everybody in the circle welcomed Lesley Fozzard by shaking her hand and introducing ourselves to the spiritual protector. We soon got onto the subject after the formalities have been completed. Helen says, "I am amazed that I have sold my waterfall within a few moments of the exhibition opening. To the Norwegian man with the strong accent. I am positive that he was the man I was speaking to on the phone before we came to the exhibition. "Lesley Fozzard says, "I did notice the tall gentleman in the middle of the room. It was very still I thought he was a statue to begin with. However, when the smoke travels around the ring and mingle with the audience, it seem to quite upset him slightly and he tried to avoid it. This just means he was trying to prevent the healing powers of the smoke. Therefore, he may have a great deal of anger within side of him. Sometimes some people have served a very troubled life and find it tough to associate and mingle with society." Two servers walk by with trays of canapés and champagne, offering them to the guests. Helen says, "Not for me thank you I need to keep a clear head." Most of the group helped themselves to another refreshing glass of champagne and a canapé or two. I must say it was a thoroughly enjoyable time with everybody in this circle. It just seemed as though everybody wanted to gather around Lesley Fozzard. Also, my wife, Helen. The evening was full of entertainment where everybody was admiring paintings and socialising in an excellent environment of goodness. I felt that everybody was getting along with each other so well; I understood it must have been the amazing powers of Lesley Fozzard spiritual cleansing. Therefore, the entertaining of the evening Roald steadily into the midnight hours where there were only a few people left behind. Charlie says, "well this seems to have been a success as over 50% of the paintings have been sold and the rest is on reserve." Is this right dear? "I have not got the final figures, yet but it seems that you are pretty much on the ball fair Charlie Honey." You are going to have a busy weekend delivering paintings. "I will be delivering a few Personally, but there are also quite a few that I will have to do FedEx as they just live so far away. " It was time to close up the function, as it was approximately 1:30 in the morning. Therefore, after the last guests had said their goodbyes, it was time for Helen and me to head off home. As they rather tiring and busy day for my wife. Helen and Charlie said their goodbyes to Carl Manson and thank their staff for their support and hard work. Helen and Charlie slipped away into the darkness of the early hours of the morning. Arm in the arm as they walked across the car park. Once again the click, click, click, of Helen's heels as they walked towards the car. Helen picture keys out of her handbag. "Darling can you drive I think I have had a little bit too much to drink," Charlie replies, "of course my dear." Charlie takes the keys of his wife and opens the passenger door. Soon Charlie was sitting in the car enjoying the drive home with his wife.

CHAPTER 6

Charlie stretched in a comfortable, Cosy bed after a recent Friday night the morning after snoozing the alarm clock already three times in a row. Suddenly realising that he has quite a severe hangover from the evening before. As the celebrations with him and his wife did not end when they arrived home. "Good morning I knew you were struggling a little bit and then I thought I would bring you an excellent fried breakfast in bed." Charlie stretches in bed one time more and yawns slightly, and begins to ask his wife for "a glass of water and aspirins." Helen says, "It is an excellent beginning of the day." As she pulled back, the curtains and the morning sunlight floods into the room. Charlie sits up in bed and starts to eat his breakfast. With a croaky voice, he states. "Thank you, honey," Helen asks Charlie, "what are your plans for today." Charlie gets a sip from his cup of coffee and replies. "I was going to take the car down for a much-needed M.O.T on Stafford Park at M.O.T's are us, "Helen replies, "you mean Rob's place M.O.T R us." " Yes, that is the place the very same place next to the new Telford motorcycle centre T.M.C What are your plans for today honey." "Well, I have to deliver my paintings. You know too that strange Australian man, the one that was standing very still and staring," Charlie says, "I have an unusual feeling concerning this man, there is something about him I think he may be ex-forces," Helen replies, "yes maybe he is. But there is nothing to worry about Darling." Helen puts Charlie at ease. Charlie starts to feel a little bit better after the glass of water and two aspirins the delicious fry up.

Charlie finishes his breakfast and his wife took the tray downstairs giving Charlie time to get dressed.

Soon Charlie was walking into the kitchen sneaking up behind his wife as She Was loading up the dishwasher. Helen stands up straight, and Charlie did not lose this chance to give his wife and nice morning cuddle. "Oh, you naughty boys there is a time and place for everything you know."

"I am just having a cuddle."

"That is where it starts soon you will have me on the kitchen floor or even on the kitchen table like last night."

"Well, I have no way of replying to that. You have got to me."

"Well yes, you will have to get going soon because the M.O.T is going to be late."

"Yes you are right gear I must get along and get the car ready I need to take it up to the car wash before I take it round for the M.O.T as Rob hates a dirty car in his workshop."

"Go on then you randy bugger get out my kitchen and do some work!"

"Honey you be careful delivering that painting."

"I will be okay don't you worry about that."

"Okay, then dear I will leave you to it let us get on."

"We get on beautifully."

"No you know what I mean, I mean that I have to get on and get the car sorted out before I take it to the M.O.T so I have to get on now. See you later."

As Charlie starts to walk out of the door grabbing his jacket and his wallet at the same time.

"Haven't you forgotten something, my dear?"

"Is it our wedding anniversary?"

"Note is definitely not our anniversary, but you have forgotten to give me a kiss."

"I thought that you did not want any hanky-panky this morning."

"No, you horny bugger I just wanted a kiss, is that not too much for me to ask for."

Charlie took two steps forward towards his wife and his wife took two steps forward to Charlie. Both met in the middle of the kitchen. Helen and Charlie gave each other a lovely morning kiss.

"You have a nice day dear," as Charlie turned round and walked out of the door. Helen picked up the telephone and gave the Australian man a courtesy call to let him know that she would be on her way soon.

Charlie walked into the double garage and opened the electric garage door. The sunlight crept across the floor and up the garage wall until the garage was flooded with beautiful late morning sunrays. Charlie took the keys out of his pocket and pushes the button to open the car door. Within moments, he had jumped into the driver's seat and started the engine. The car rolled out of the garage as Charlie pushes the button to close the garage door behind him. Charlie looked out of the window of the car watching his wife waving him goodbye. As Charlie drove off the driveway onto the side road. Steadily but powerfully pulled away from his house.

Soon he was at Telford town centre petrol station after a quick spurt up the Eastern primary.

"That will be £65 please sir."

"Oh, by the way, may I have a deluxe car wash, please."

"That will be £75, please." Charlie paid by his contactless Barclaycard and grabbed his receipt Thank you he said. Please help yourself the words he heard when he was walking out of the petrol station through the shop. "Hello Charlie, "a gentleman recognised Charlie from the exhibition. " How did the Art exhibition go last night Charlie?" Charlie replies, "I am in quite a bit of a rush, but it went very well last night. As my wife was very pleased with the sales." The man replied, "Well I am very happy with that it was a fabulous exhibition. " Charlie said, "well I will be very sure that I make sure that I tell my wife the next time I see her this evening. I must dash. "Charlie made a hasty escape out of the petrol station. Not that he was really interested all bothered about the bloke but he just really needed to get to this M.O.T station on time. It was going to take 15 minutes sitting in the car wash so left Charlie five minutes to drive from Telford town centre to Stafford-park just leaving him just enough time to make it through the traffic.

Charlie briskly walked across the petrol forecourt and jumped in his Mercedes-Benz. Then he smoothly drove the car round to the car wash. Putting a CD in Turning off the radio at the same time. Retrieving the electric aerial to avoid any damage to it on the car radio telescopic antenna. Then he drove forward in between the curbs up to a mini console. Soon he had stopped typing in the five figures serial codes that the receptionist had given him. The red lights went out on the car wash display board and a green light illuminated. Charlie rolled the car steadily into the car wash. Soon the windscreen was covered in foamy bubbles and the car wash started to do its magic. Charlie reminisced about the good old times when he used to go through the car wash with his father. Charlie felt a little sad feeling creep over him. I know today, I should not really let this bother me, but God damage it does. A small voice as a thought came into his head and said, "Charlie do not use his name in vain." He thinks of those words today. As Charlie remembers as they are the words of his father and suddenly Charlie starts to feel a great deal better from these loving memories of his father. It was such a comforting feeling. Happy Thoughts and good memories at that. Charlie shouts the words out loud «God bless you, Dad, God bless you.» safe in the comfort this Charlie knew the sound of the car wash will drown out his praise outside the car wash. Praise the Lord.

Before long, Charlie was driving out the tracks of the car wash. He pulled over and jumped out of the car to check for any marks or dents on the car and cleaned his wiper blade rubbers with his thumbnail and a cloth. A quick glimpse at his watch. Exactly five to. I shall make it if there is no trouble with the traffic on the island. Because of the road works.

Before long, Charlie was there. "Hello, Rob just coming for my booking for the M.O.T," Rob says, "yes just park it over there in the M.O.T allocated station parking bay. " Rob turned around and walked back into the garage workshop. Charlie parked the car, walked into the reception, and handed over the car keys to the receptionist. She said, "If you come back in roughly one hour, she shall be ready for you. " Charlie responded, "thank you dear." In addition, as simple as that Charlie turned round, walked out of the office, and walked around next door to throw a look at the motorcycle centre. It did not take long for Charlie to arrive into the motorcycle centre, as it is only next-door. Charlie opened the doorway and could smell the luscious leather immediately. An elegant looking woman said, "Can I assist you, sir." I am just browsing Charlie replied. Charlie had a meander around the shop part looking at the new leather jackets. Well, they are a fair price I could have one for my wife and myself. Charlie picks up two jackets for the proper size of him and his wife. He tries his on and looks in the mirror and Wow does that look fresh. The woman from behind the counter said, "that certainly suits you, sir." Charlie replied confidently. "Yes, this new range actually looks serious. My wife also would like a jacket." So Charlie bought himself and his wife beautiful leather jacket something casual to ride the bike with.

Charlie paid with his credit card. I think you have made a mistake on the price here my dear?" " No, I have not certainly they are on special offer and if you purchase yourself one and your wife one you get a discount as simple as that. If you have brought your wife in with you, we may have yet thrown in matching sweatbands. "But instead you will barely have to make do with a free coffee how does that sound, sir." "Yes, that will be lovely." "Well, the coffee machine is just around the corner good you can help yourself." Charlie walked off around the corner, began to pour himself a delicious coffee, and sat down on the stool. Using the time to catch up on his Facebook friends. Charlie reads, a motorcycle rally meets at Iron Bridge on Sunday. It might be nice for my wife and I want to get out on that run. Well, I do not think so; I guess we will just go out for a ride by ourselves. Charlie then just browses through these messages seeing if there is anything interesting going on. No, not really it is just the same kind of thing. Charlie's phone rings. "Hello" Hello, Charlie, it's Glenn sorry I did not call you on my regular mobile, but I am at the office." " Is everything alright?" " Yes, it is everything has played out perfectly well." " That is respectable."

"So does that mean we can retire or even have a break?" "I would not say just at the moment, but we are becoming very close to it." "That is good then, I will keep my eye out for something novel." "Well, yes, please do that, that's good Charlie I will do the same at my terminal." "Well, Glenn I have found a new motorcycle shop in Telford. It is a fabulous new range of blade motorcycle leather jackets and the canvas jackets. And they are all definitely having the right price." Glenn asks, do they have any all in black. Yes, perhaps they may have been scattered. "Why? " Considerably, I just thought as I could do with some new gear. "Well, you will only have to get on down one day and find out for yourself." "Well, I will simply have to do that sometime next week." "Good idea Glenn that will be a good time to meet up." "Great Charlie okay well I will see you sometime next week gotta go now catch up with you afterwards." Glenn ended the call.

Charlie stood up and had another browse around the shop he walked around the corner and found that in that location was an inspection window where he sat down and watched the motorcycle mechanics performing an M.O.T on a fire blade motorcycle. The young man walked around the motorbike with a tablet computer in his hand checking the motorcycle for any imperfections. The young man was working very proficiently on this bike. Checking the tyres, brakes, and everything for the M.O.T. Right at that moment. The M.O.T engineer looked up at Charlie looking through the windowpane. He taps the peak of his cap politely. Charlie replied with a nod as usual motorcyclists do in respect of riders. The young operate roles a motorcycle off the testing ramp and returned it back with a row of other bikes. Through the shutters, Charlie could see a very professional team of motorcycle mechanics working very hard on two or three motorcycles within the workshop. A pleasant manner to pass some time Charlie was thinking. Charlie noticed that the motorcycle shop and workshop were superbly clean not like any other motorcycle shops that he had been before. The service here just seemed the best. The M.O.T engineer walked over to the large shutter doors and open them with a key. The roller shutter doors opened and the young man ducked underneath the Roller shutter and walked out into the car park. A few moments after a large white van reversed up to the doors. The young man opened the back of the doors and rolled out a large ramp. Sane, the man, rolled up into the van three motorcycles. He was in the van for a couple of minutes I suppose it was just tying the bikes down. Just getting them ready for delivery. Soon the roller shutter closed behind the van. Soon, Charlie could hear the van pull away. Charlie walked over to the young woman behind the desk and asked the question "do you execute a delivery service here." "Yes we do, we pick up and deliver your bike. For services and notices, etc."

Charlie replied, "Will that seems to be an excellent service for the people that do not find the time as they are hard-working in the day."

Charlie says, "Will thank you for your time and your service. I am sure I will bring my BMW into here one day soon as your shop certainly looks a professional outfit."

The young woman behind the counter replied, "we will be more than happy to do you a full service on your motorcycle whenever it is necessary."

Charlie spoke politely, "may I leave my jackets here for a few moments while I pop out to get something to eat from the burger bar outside."

"Yes, of course, hand them over here I will put them safely away for you sir."

Charlie handed over the two leather jackets and said, "thank you." Then Charlie strolled out of the shop and walked up to the burger bar just outside the motorcycle shop. There was quite a gathering of motorcyclists outside and more were turning up as Charlie was walking towards the burger van. Charlie could overhear the motorcyclist talking about their ride out from Quote. "Yes, sir, can I help you." A woman asks from behind the counter in the burger bar. Charlie says, "a cheese and onion burger please." Charlie hands over some loose change and pays for his burger. Then just stands there quietly, waiting for the burger to be cooked. Charlie cannot help overhearing what the motorcyclists were talking about describing the fund that they hand out on the road this morning. "The original burger Sir." The woman behind the counter handed it to Charlie. His burger is all wrapped up nice and neat in silver foil. Charlie is fussy where he eats, especially at burger bars. Charlie had a good look around the burger bar and notice that it was spotless too. There were no funny greasy smells in the air. Therefore, Charlie decided to bite into his delicious cheese and onion burger. The taste of the burger was fresh and probably one of the finest burgers that he had ever eaten from a burger van. Charlie just stood there quietly eating. While looking at the fabulous display of highly polished motorcycles. Charlie just likes to be the grey man as they say. Standing still quietly but listening and watching everything. Charlie's phone buzzes in his pocket. It was a text message from the M.O.T's R us car garage. "M.O.T is complete." A simple but effective text message. Charlie finished a few mouthfuls of his burger and through the rubbish in the bin. Then he walked around the corner straight up to the M.O.T office, picked up his keys, and paid for his MOT service. "You do not have any reminders they ran straight through with your M.O.T no problems good for another year," Charlie replied, "thank you very much." The young woman smiled from behind the counter and Charlie replied with a smile back. Charlie turned around and walked out of the door and soon he was back in his

Mercedes-Benz a quick look around the cockpit of the car. Everything seems to be in order. An excellent job, Charlie says while patting his steering wheel. As most men do talk to their cars, you know. Charlie pulls away, drives off the car park, pulls up outside the burger bar, and walks into the motorcycle centre. "Hello, have you come for your jackets?"

"Yes thank you I have. Thank you very much for looking after them for me." " No problem, all part of the service." The lovely young woman hands over the two jackets back to Charlie. "Thank you." Then Charlie turned around and walked out of the doorway. A quick press of his key fob and the boot popped open. Charlie placed the leather goods in the boot and closed it securely shut. While I was walking close to, the side of the car he nodded to the man motorcyclists and they all nodded back. The good thing about riders is that they will always help anyone 90% of motorcyclists go to a bunch of charities raising fundraising events. Yes, rider raises money for charity in a meaningful manner. So the next time you consider a rider on the road. Give him or hear the room.

Charlie drove away from the car park steadily. In addition, headed home. By the time, he got home his wife was not there. Therefore, he just parked the car in the garage. And decided to tinker and clean his motorcycle and also do the services on his motorcycle and his wife's these things have to be regularly done cleaning and oiling the chain checking all the fluids etc. and a good coat of shiny polish over all the panels. Keep your motorcycle in showroom condition. Nobody really wants to look at the dirty bike. Let alone write one. This took most of the day, as Charlie felt quite relaxed cleaning the bike listening to some good music. After this, Charlie went up into the kitchen, grabs some apples, and took them down to his old horse. It is a beautiful treat for Smith's as he does love a good Bromley Apple is also partial to a few polo mints.

Charlie leans over the five bar gate and whistles. Soon Smith's trots up straight up to the gate. "What a pal you are Smith's." by the sparkle in the horse's eyes and the prick of his ears. Charlie could see that he was very healthy and very pleased to see him. Smith's gives Charlie a little nudge with his nose. He could feel the smooth softness of his nose as Charlie petted him. Just like a big dog. A scratch behind the ear just seems to do the trick. In addition, Charlie starts to feed his big pet with the Bromley apples. Smith's just bites them in half and juicy apples make a very happy crunching noise for my horse. After the apples are finished. Charlie climbs up onto the five bars gate and gets onto the bare back of his horse. And lies down on top of him. The horse just takes a steady little stroll around the paddock with Charlie relaxing on his back. The warm feeling of the horse Charlie could feel this. This is just a beautiful feeling relaxing on the back of a horse walking around letting the horse doing its own thing. Charlie does this quite regularly. As it is thinking space. In addition, the horse is quite comfortable with Charlie relaxing on his back. Occasionally Charlie has fallen asleep totally and stayed there until the early hours of the morning. It is amazing and wildlife you actually see standing while lying down on the back of a horse. Charlie must have been lying on there for at least two hours. Alternatively, maybe even three. Time just slipped by. Soon Charlie could hear a car pulling up on the drive. That must be his wife. Therefore, Charlie gives the horse attack to walk over towards the gate. In addition, obediently Smith's walks over towards the gate. Charlie dismounts and walked up the hill towards the house. Just catching a glimpse of his wife walking into the house. Charlie was soon at the front door. And walking into the house. "Hello darling, "there is no answer so Charlie called out once more. A little bit louder this time. "Hello, darling," She replies this time shouting from upstairs. "I am in the shower, honey." Charlie decides to make you a nice coffee and makes his wife one. Charlie stood there in the kitchen waiting for the kettle to boil preparing the cups. Soon he had made two drinks and started drinking his own. Knowing that his wife would be down in a minute. But not this time. She was taking lot longer than usual. In addition, her coffee started to go cold. As Charlie had already finished his. He noticed a magazine on the table. In addition, started to browse up on it. A fantastic painting was one of the original grandmasters. That was worth an absolute fortune. Soon his wife came downstairs in her robe. In addition, walk straight into the living room and sat down. Charlie thought this was quite unusual usually she would actually say something to him. Charlie decided to make a fresh coffee. In addition, carried it into the living room where she was sitting. She seemed quite withdrawn not attempting to say anything. Charlie said to his wife. "Here is an excellent fresh coffee for you." Just put it on a table dear."

Charlie quietly placed a drink on the table and walked back into the kitchen. Wondering what was wrong with his wife. Things started to turn over in his mind. It is not like her to have a shower straight away when she comes in. Charlie picked up the magazine from in the kitchen, walked back into the living room, and sat down on one of the comfortable chairs. He looked at the magazine that was open to the page that his wife had been looking at.

In addition, read just a little bit about the painting. A few minutes passed in silence between the couple. Helen finally decides to sit up and take a sip out of her coffee cup. "Thank you, dear," she says. Charlie replies, "been a busy day honey." Yes, I am very shattered it has been a hard day today. I am definitely going to bed early tonight." Then Helen looks over to Charlie and smiles.

She says, "I see you have seen my magazine."

"Yes, I have seen rather an interesting article about a new painting that has been bought in Shropshire."

"Yes, dear that now belongs to the Australian gentleman that was at the art exhibition the other night. He has brought the old Manor house in Shropshire. In addition, he is filling it with antiques and works of art. However, this one painting that he has shown me is worth £10 million. He has bought it as well-done investment and a little bit of a tax fiddle. "Charlie thought of this to be absorbing. The old Manor house he thinks. That is a little bit close for comfort, but I will have to work something out. "Are you enjoying your coffee, honey?"

"Yes thank you. The waterfall painting that he bought off me you wanted me to hang it for him when I delivered it to the house. Anyway, I do not want to talk about it because I am too tired." In addition, Helen stood up and started to walk, "I am going to bed now."

"Okay, good night then honey." His wife walked over to him and gives Charlie a little kiss on the cheek. And then walked out of the room.

I am saying she did look rather tired. Charlie picked up the remote control, turned on the television, and started to watch the 9 o'clock news. Soon, Charlie, himself was dozing in the seat. Half an hour later the Nine O'clock News had finished. In addition, it was time to watch a lovely film. So Charlie Flick through the channels and finds a beautiful romantic movie to watch all by himself. The movie was about a man who had fallen in love with a woman in the past. The only way they contacted each of them was through letters and a letterbox. Yes, it was a seriously good movie. Soon it was time for Charlie to go to bed and he called up the wooden stairs late at night. And Slipped into the bed beside his wife. Charlie is lying on the bed thinking. As his head was sinking into the pillows. Moreover, his wife was lying next to him softly breathing. "This could be the final painting what Glenn was talking about the one that would make his free." So anyway tomorrow that is what we are going to have to arrange. Soon Charlie drifted off to sleep.

* * *

——————————— Sunday morning ———————————

Charlie and Helen almost woke up together this morning. "Good morning dear."

"Good morning Honey."

"It is a lovely beautiful sunny morning it is just perfect for a nice ride out on the bikes." Helen stares into Charlie's eyes, and says, "Can you make me drink, please."

"Of course my dear. You stay in bed and wait there I will get you your breakfast and coffee." soon Charlie was up and out of bed and heading into the kitchen to prepare his wife's and breakfast, in his dressing gown. Charlie things now would be a good idea to give his wife a new present the matching motorcycle jacket that he had bought from T.M.C. To Charlie went out to the car while the kettle was boiling and collected the two jackets from the car. Charlie then carried the jackets upstairs and places them outside the bedroom door. Then sneaked back downstairs to collect the breakfast that he had prepared. He then carried the breakfast tray upstairs and into the bedroom. "Good morning honey, here is your breakfast. " Charlie stood by the side of the bed holding the tray and Helen adjusted herself and sat up in the bed. "Thank you dear" Charlie kicked off his slippers, sat on the bed, and started to enjoy his breakfast in bed with his wife. It is not very often they get a chance to sit together in bed as both of them have very demanding jobs. "Darling you have many delicious scrambled egg on toasts just how I like it." I am so glad that you are enjoying it."

"So how do you fancy taking the motorbikes out today for a nice long run, maybe we can go out and visit some friends or just take a ride out by ourselves what do you think?"

"Yes that would be so nice I miss my BMW, and it has been so long since we have managed to ride out together. As long as the weather is good today."

"Yes honey I do believe it is going to be an excellent day for today."

Charlie just finishes and put the tray down on the bedside table and slips on his slippers and walks towards the door. "Where are you going, darling?"

"Just give me a moment to dear." Charlie leans out of the door and picks up the two bags with the leather jackets inside. "There you go dear a nice present for you."

"For me darling?"

Charlie hands over the plastic bag. Helen's face lights up with a lovely smile. One for me and one for you Charlie say. Helen pulls the leather jacket out of the plastic bag and she is over the moon with her new leather jacket. Instantly she hops out of bed and start to try it on. While she is standing and looking into the mirror, Charlie pulls on his own jacket as well. Why don't we just look delicious together? Helen pulled her zip up halfway but was still showing an impressive cleavage. "Oh yes, they look so rather good." Helen grabs hold of Charlie and gives him a big kiss and a Hogg. "All these beautiful matching pair of jackets are going to make you and I stand out in the crowd when we are out on our ride out today."

Charlie says, "Will come then dear let us get going and get downstairs and organise our root out for the day."

"Wonderful" as excitable Helen said as she is jumping up and down.

40 minutes later and they are both downstairs dressed in a biker's gear waiting to go into the garage just get the bike started. A last-minute check of each other's equipment and

Charlie and Helen walk out to the garage. Helen says, "Have you cleaned my bike for me,"

"Yes I have five made sure everything is perfect and it is nice and shiny for you. " Alan leans forward and looks into the petrol tank Charlie could see the shiny reflection of her helmet in the petrol tank. Feeling quite pleased with his hard work. Charlie and Helen together put the keys into the ignition and start the bikes. The power of the two motorcycles ticking over in the garage felt quite spectacular. Charlie sets up the Bluetooth between the two motorcycle helmets. "Can you hear me darling testing. Testing 123."

"Yes, I can honey loud and clear."

Helen says, "It is my turn to pick the music, and you can just do the navigation, Charlie. " Charlie gives his bike a little blip of the throttle. The bike revs up smoothly crisply cleanly. In addition, Helen does the same. Helen and Charlie mount their motorcycles. Charlie says to Helen, "Are you ready to go."

She says, "let us go!" Charlie and Helen together roles their motorcycles out of the garage, and Charlie pushes the button on his motorcycle to close the garage doors. The large double garage doors smoothly close. In addition, they are both drive down to the side main road and accelerate away.

http://www.rms.nsw.gov.au/documents/roads/licence/motorcycle-riders-handbook.pdf

"Are you comfortable the."

"Yes," – – "where are we going."

"I thought it would be nice to travel out through Newport and go to market Drayton. What do you make of that honey?"

"That will be excellent."

Helen and Charlie are riding accelerating and cutting the groove round the country lanes. Oh, it is just so nice been able to get out onto the open road once more. The power of these BMW RRS thousand cc motorcycles is awesome. The first of many bends appear quite quickly. In addition, Charlie decides to get his knee down around the bend and his wife Helen soon follows a nice steady long curve. Charlie looks over his shoulder and sees his wife's motorcycle leaned over entirely and her knee touching the ground exactly on the same line as Charlie. "Wow that was excellent," Helen said. Very clearly into the microphone. Charlie replied by saying, "we have a very nice long straight in front of us, let us go for it."

"You leader I will follow." Charlie pulls back on the throttle and opens up the powerful motorcycle by changing gear one after the other. As Charlie glances at the speedometer 60, 70, mph and the bike is still accelerating. "Open clear then the approaching to the right," as soon as Charlie mentioned this he was on it and around the bend and his wife followed. Back onto a nice straight, Charlie calls out his wife, "would you like to take the leader and head for Newport?"

"Of course, coming through." Charlie eases over to the right-hand side slightly to let his wife whizzed past. Charlie spotted her in his right-hand mirror as she approached that speed to overtake safely.

"No junctions ahead a straight road come on through." his wife pinned the throttle and zipped past Charlie like the one he was standing still. This brought out the inner feeling within the riders and soon they were dancing through the narrow streets heading towards Newport accelerating excessive speeds of 60 to 120 miles an hour. Within 10 minutes, they were heading towards Newport high Street. They did not stop in the high Street just drove very slow around 20 miles an hour through the town. Charlie and Helen do not like Newport. However, Newport does not really like motorcyclists. In addition, there is no shops or cafes that accommodate motorcyclists. However, there is a lovely stretch of road heading over the canal out of the back of Newport past the church. About 800 m after the canal there is a turning on the right-hand side and 10 m pass that there is a turning on the left hand side. This is the best road to take if you just want to check you ride out and give it a real road test. As the roads down there are pretty, clear and not many cars take that high-speed twisty road. Helen indicates with her hand for Charlie to overtake, Charlie knocks it down a gear and pushes his foot on the back brake slightly with a little bit more acceleration with the throttle. Charlie pops a weakly straight past his wife 60 m on the back wheel as Charlie accelerates. Now Charlie is pole position and his wife is following up from the rear. Coming out of the back end of Newport. Past a large church on the bend on the left-hand side near the main road junction. Charlie and Helen appear at the junction together. They both make sure that it is clear. Using full concentration looking as far down the road as possible the left and right-hand arcs of visibility. Also listening out for traffic. The road is clear so that both accelerate out checking over their shoulder as they meet. A clear road but this road just likes the police for some reason.

Therefore, they both keep it nice and steady on the speed limit. About 5 to 6 miles down the road there is a turning off the right-hand fork to market Drayton make sure you take it honey do not miss it. Coming up to, the petrol station on the right-hand side there is a beautiful long sweeping left-hand bend, "Helen here is your favourite band." Helen loves this bend because she can get her knee down very smoothly and it happens to be the first bend that she ever got her knee down on. "Here we go." Helen calls out. "Fabulous." as her knee is down and she is sweeping around the bend cutting the groove. In addition, Charlie followed at Max speed for that bend. They both came out of the bend as clear as a bell; it was such an exhilarating feeling as they swept around the bend. "Right, honey that turning is on the right-hand side in about half a mile."

"Okay".

"Are you having fun dear?"

"I am having the time of my life."

"Was not that bends just a moment ago absolutely awesome. " Charlie replies, "awesome my dear – no concentrate because the turning is coming up," Charlie starts to indicate right. He looks over his shoulder all you can see is his wife. He looks clear in front of him and there is not think in front of him. Therefore, Charlie takes the turning up the slip road. In addition, his wife follows him. "Okay all clear,"

"Absolutely my dear entirely, let us goes for it." In addition, both of the BMWs accelerate straight down the main road. This is a beautiful country lane. Plenty of twists on this lane. Helen and Charlie soon waltzing through the lanes and all of the twisty bits. "Time for some music Helen," Helen pushes the buttons to bring up the music that she has chosen already on her MP3 player. "Wow, this is interesting, who is this fabulous artist."

Helen replied, "It is I," Charlie said, "I have never heard of these before." Helen said, "No it is I," Charlie said, "No-no, I have not even heard of them before either. They must be one of them, German bands. However, they are exquisite. "Helen laughed loudly down the microphone and said,» no you soon believes me,» Charlie replied laugh with a chortle. «Now I understand as I am. Now I realize you sound excellent. How did you manage to do that?»

"So you do love it then well I will tell you I used your fancy keyboard."

"Well, I think it is perfect and complete music it is for motorcycling. So let us ride baby," the two motorcycles ripped up the road in perfect harmony heading straight towards market Drayton. Increasingly twisty bends Charlie could see the church steeple. In the centre of town time to ease off they both think. In addition, take a nice steady cruise into town. "Let us find a coffee shop darling sweet one this time."

"I know just the spot right next to the market. " This is the market Charlie really wanted to go to because this is where he picks up his mobile phones from. One they are obliging and cheap and to the shop assistant are not asked for his name and address when he buys them. A perfect burning mobile phone. I will buy two of them and then I can post the other one to my friends Glenn. Charlie and Helen pull up outside the coffee shop. They soon park up their motorcycles within a group of other motorcycles. "Dismount."

"Your turn for the coffee's darling,"

"Look, my dear, I will always buy you drink there is no problem about that. Coffee is it."

"Yes please, darling I will go and find somewhere to sit outside."

Charlie disappears off into the rooms through the door and into the cafe. Helen found somewhere very nice to sit outside under just a bit of shade so we do not cook in the sun. Helen places her helmet on the table along with Charlie's helmet. Helen unzips her leather jacket halfway down. I know what you are all thinking you are thinking wow she is showing her boobs again. Quite the contrary she does wear T-shirts you know. After 5 or 10 minutes, Charlie was soon out of the coffee shop carrying two mugs of coffee. Admiring his wife as he approaches with the drinks. It did not take long for somebody to start respecting our twin BMW RRS 1000 motorcycles on the car park. You could see them looking. It was a good feeling it is nice to see one BMW RRS 1000. However, two. Together? With one digit difference, on the number plates. Now that is skill. Charlie continues drinking his coffee with his wife. Soon we are starting to see a new and other friends begin to appear. As there is full respect within the motorcycling community to your wife. It is a very safe place to be with your wife. Especially if she is a motorcyclist. Because everybody looks out for everybody else.

In addition, we always believe in saying the good things and leaving the bad stuff. That is why motorcyclists have so many good friends. Soon Tex, Skip, Rambo, and Dodge, appear on our table. Then we actually start to enjoy the morning. Texas is just so funny. He just cracks so many good jokes and he is definitely leader rider. Work that one out. "Yes, bikers have their own nicknames."

Helen says, "So where have you all been today."

"Well we have just had a big ride out from the horseshoe pass which was excellent," Charlie says, "all of you went up to the pon da roaster, coffee shop." Yes and we went up to the old folks home and raised £500 this morning. Just to help out with the old dears."

Helen says, "Well-done lads raising all that money, £500! For the old folks is perfect for them. It will certainly help to their cause to raise enough money to buy the Whirlpool that they are all saving up for."

In addition, the conversation goes on similar to this. As of the above.

Therefore, we all sat there for about an hour talking about motorcycles and many other exciting things that we get up to. Charlie spoke to Helen would you like to come out for a little walk around the market. "Of course my darling. In addition, the happy couple both walked off to the market.

Charlie managed to find the market stall that he was looking for to by the burner phones. Moreover, Helen managed to buy some of her favourite things also. As they have excellent art and crafts, whilst Helen was browsing her favourite stall,

Charlie managed to escape for a few moments and look at the market stall that interested him whilst leaving Helen there to do her shopping. For her brushes and oil paints. Charlie also bought an envelope and posted the one burner mobile phone first class to Glenn. After programming in the new telephone burner number of his cell phone and Charlie also saved the appropriate number into his own burner cell phone. The code word is cell. These phones do not have any GPS location on them, but they are traceable if the mobile phone number is known or even the ISBN number of even one of the phones. Once the phone is activated the location of that phone is traceable but only at the point of the phone call. As Charlie is walking back from the post box, Helen was looking for Charlie around stalls. Charlie managed to sneak behind her Once again and be tended to follow her. Getting closer and closer until he was right behind. A perfect moment and opportunity arranged itself as Helen calls out to Charlie. Calling loudly because she cannot see him. "Charlie!"

Charlie speaks out quietly inches away from behind her ear, "here I am love." Helen literally jumped out of her skin, but she kept herself composed. "How long have you been there?" Charlie replies to her, "long enough."

"I have just walked past the donut store. Would you like some?"

"Oh yes they would be lovely darling, but not too many for me, please."

"Charlie says come on then let us go, and get some doughnuts."

"Oh, you certainly know how to look after a lady Charlie," Helen says as she is fishing for a compliment.

Darling "What has no beginning and no end and nothing in the middle?"

"I have no idea honey, what has no beginning and no end and nothing in the middle"

Charlie says, out loud "A doughnut!" they both cheerfully laugh out loud, amongst the crowd of people hustling for a bargain.

The happy couple both laughed out loud as they were walking to the donut shop.

Helen says, "My turn, what's a tree's favourite drink?"

Charlie replies, "I do not know what is trees favourite drink?"

Helen Says, "Root beer." Charlie roars out with laughter as he thinks it is so funny, "that was a good one love."

Charlie says, "Okay then why did the doughnut shop close? I do not know Darling. Why did the doughnut shop close?

Charlie answers, "The owner got tired of the hole business!"

Now they both turn up to the doughnuts stall giggling out loud to themselves.

There were lucky there was no queue. Charlie and Helen walked straight up to the window.

The smells of fresh sugared doughnuts were divine. Charlie asked, for "ten doughnuts please,"

Helen asks the man serving, "Do you have any of that delicious strawberry icing?"

"Yes I do dear we sell it in the tubs would you like one?"

"Yes, we will have one that will do very nice thank you."

The gentleman pours the creamy, delicious looking icing topping into a little tub and fits the lid on nice and firmly. Charlie pays for the doughnuts and the gentleman hands him a bag of 10 fresh doughnuts and one small tub of pink icing. The bag felt so warm in Charlie's hand, as they do not want to refresh and made that moment.

Charlie and Helen could hear a strict busker playing some music, "darling that will be a lovely place to eat our doughnuts."

"You are so right my dear."

And soon they were there listening to the music helping themselves to the delicious sweet doughnuts with a sweet strawberry icing topping. Charlie remarked "Doughnuts al dente." Helen turned and looked at Charlie while she still has her finger in her mouth as if she was sucking the icing off her finger. Looking so sexy as ever.

Charlie just dived into the doughnut bag once more and took out one fresher one. Then offered the bag to Helen. "Thank you," Helen plunged her hand into a crinkly bag of doughnuts, pulling one out bejewelled in sugar. "Thank you love!" soon Helen and Charlie manage to munch their way through 10 doughnuts and a tub of pink strawberry flavoured icing. Of which went so well with the doughnuts. 20 sticky fingers an empty paper bag later and 5 pounds lighter for a tip to the Brilliant entertainment busker. It was time to head out for another ride.

A short walk back to the coffee shop to pick up the bikes. There was still quite a crowd of people outside the coffee shop. But Helen and Charlie took no time to jump on their bikes and ride off.

The ride-outs took most of the day as we visited many little towns and villages on the way to coffee shops etc.. Until we ended up at Halfpenny Green Airport. Just to watch the sunset with a nice cup of coffee with my good wife. My wife and I had this lovely meal at the airport restaurant. I must say, the food there is delicious. "Do you not you think so my darling." Absolutely.

All that is left to do now is the nice long ride home. "How would you like to go home honey would you like to take the twisties?" "I would like to take the fastest route home darling as I have had enough for today darling." a fast-track ride straight home it is then".

CHAPTER 7

"Monday morning is such a drag don't you think so honey?" "Well, I believe, so but I think that your job is lot more intense than mine being a GP Doctor." Helen slides an early morning cup of coffee over the island towards Charlie. "Maybe this will make you feel a little bit better darling." "It will thank you, honey." Charlie ponders through his iPhone to check out the weather prognosis. Just to assure if the weather is good enough to ride the bike into work today. The weather looks good, but there are showers in the afternoon. "I suppose I will risk it?" "Pardon me, dear." "No, honey, it is just me, I am merely thinking out loud again. The weather is not going to be too good this afternoon. There looks like there is going to be a light shower this afternoon." "Well, you are going to have to make your mind up which vehicle to used today. If it is the car you are going to have to leave now because you know how long it takes to puzzle through the traffic jams." "You are so thoughtful honey, I am going to take the motorbike I am sure it will be all good. It will render me a little bit more time to you." "Well, in that case, you can give me hand to load the car." "Well, yes, of course, what is it you require putting in the car?" "Just those bags and boxes over there. I have had a little bit of a clear out and I need to bring these down to the charity shop." Charlie takes a nice long sip from his coffee cup and looks into his wife's eyes.

"I will do this for you, honey." Charlie then quickly rose up out of his seat from the kitchen island and walked straight to the bags piled up in the living room and started to carry them out to the car. "Dear you do not have to do it right now because your coffee will become cold." "Know you are all good honey, it will only take me a minute, and so I can just spend another five minutes with you before I have to leave for work." "Oh thank you dear. I will just make you some toast, is that okay?" "Marmalade please I will be fine thank you, you are a darling." Charlie is soon piling the two boxes into the car boot also the large black bin bags onto the back seat of his wife's car, after a few journeys back and forth. Charlie soon finishes his task and returns to the kitchen.

"Your toast is ready!"

"Thank you my dear."

Charlie just gives a QuickTime check on his oyster Rolex watch.

"You genuinely love your present don't you from me darling?"

"Yes, it is fabulous. And an incredible gift, I love it." Helen smiled sweetly, and rolls back her long hair with her fringes and tuck it behind her ear with her finger. Charlie bites into his marmalade on toast with a crunch. Helen proceeds to tidy up the kitchen. "I too do love my leather jacket that you brought me. It matches the bike absolutely perfectly.

Also fits me perfectly divine." "Well, I saved the receipt just in case it did not suit you." "Will you can just hand that receipt over to your accountant we will not be changing this jacket," she beamed with a sexy smile. Something suddenly caught Charlie's attention outside to the back garden. "Look at this!" "Where in the backyard?" "Yes, but look upwards." Charlie and Helen walked close to the window view out over the terrace into the large garden. "Look In the sky" above the backyard trees there was a mass of starlings flying around just out of sight disappeared behind the trees. Then suddenly they made a grand entrance making unusual shapes in the sky right above our garden "they just look so beautiful," Helen said. "Free as a Bird or not they." Charlie and Helen admire starlings flying around in the sky. While Charlie is still enjoying his last piece of toast and marmalade. "I quite fancy a holiday, do you want to pick out some catalogues today's honey, so we can have a mini-break or something like that." Excitedly Helen jumps up and down slightly wildly and giving her husbands a big hug showing her appreciation. "Just make certain it is all-inclusive in a villa somewhere. So we can loosen up in the sunshine. By a pool." "Oh so lovely me and you together in the wilderness." "Well if you put it like that honey, yes, it sounds delightful." Charlie checks the time on his Rolex once more. "Well darling, I must get going now time is fleeting." Helen put her arms around Charlie and gives him a big kiss. "And says thank you." Charlie pulled her in tightly and gives her a little bit of a ravishing, in front of the large windows. "Come on darling you do not have enough time for this." "Tonight I will do something really special for you." "Am' I on a promise for this evening?" "Absolutely my darling." "But now you have to get going you are going to be late, and I do not want you to be driving like a LEGEND on that motorbike."

"I will do dear, you know that I will be all right."

"You are a skilled rider, it is just all the other people on the roads, cars, and things."

"I totally understand darling I will keep my buffers, nice and large for you."

"Well thank you, honey, I am going now,"

The couple blew each other a kiss as Charlie was walking out through the kitchen grabbing his motorbike leathers at the same time. Charlie soon disappeared through the kitchen door through into the garage. He turns on the lights, the twinkling sound of the fluorescent tubes click blink and flash as they were lighting up.

This is such a lovely sound. But soon he was getting ready and opening the garage door. Letting the overcast early-morning sunlight flood into the garage. Within a couple of minutes, Charlie is dressed on his bike and heading out of the garage down the drive with a wave to his wife. But the some reason she was not there this morning. Charlie thought nothing of it as it is Monday morning, and she does have her things to sort out maybe she was on the telephone.

Soon on the busy motorway driving steady on very crowded roads. He rode fast under the motorway island at Shifnal. That is unusual I must be a little bit later than usual, as I have not seen my bike a mate.

Continuing cruises down the motorway and hits a small piece of clear road. Just before the Cannock junction, so Charlie opens it up slightly. A big gusty breeze catches

Charlie's motorcycle and pushes it out off his line. At that moment, a long wheelbase van comes steaming past the inside Lane of him. And luckily enough shelters Charlie's motorcycle enough from the Gusting Wind. Charlie battled with his motorcycle for a moment before the long wheelbase van acted as a windbreak. Charlie took this all in his stride, though. Just a little bit of counter steering to avoid a rather serious collision. On the motorway. Now Charlie filtered and joined up onto the M6 and the wind is now facing a different direction. But he is still aware of the blustering powerful wind. And keeps an eye on the treetops and bushes for an early warning signal of the gusting whether crossing the motorway flapping the leaves and bending trees to give an early warning sign of the dangers ahead.

Besides, this the motorway journey all the way down to London was pretty uneventful and a very pleasant and delightful ride down to his London practice. And he was soon in the building saying hello to his secretary and putting an Order in for his early morning cup of coffee. Before Charlie knew it, the first client of the morning was walking through the door.

"Take a seat Mrs plumb bob."

Charlie secretly giggling about her silly name. Her parents must have been so cruel.

"So how can I help you today?"

Well, that is pretty much how the Monday morning started, I know work is so boring but when I get the right people in my office, I do not mind. I use little things to entertain myself with my patients. As they say, it helps pass the time of the day and brings a smile to my patients. As they say, a happy patient is a healthy patient.

Soon finished off writing my reports for the morning practice. And subtly sneak out on my lunch break. One block down the road and he disappear down the subway Tube, he walks down the steep escalators as fast as he can do, and deep underground he runs and is soon standing on the platform. Standing still in the shadows waiting for the Tube train to appear. He feels the wind of the train coming up the tunnel. And the squeak of the brakes as the train slows down in the underground station. Charlie waits for the last moment before he boards the train. He just makes it through the doors. Perfect. Just make sure that nobody was following him. Charlie sits down and starts to read his newspaper really just only to blend in also to obscure his face. He was only on this train for one stop along the line. The train grinds to a halt. And Charlie once again waits to the last moment till he jumps off the train. Charlie checks left and right up the platform. It is all clear. Then he proceeds to leave the train station up the escalators and out of the underground. He strolls casually over to a telephone box and dials the memorised phone number. Charlie speaks the code word "cell, "a deep voice confirms the password and replies, "five minutes I will meet you at the usual." Charlie says, "I confirm that." Charlie places the handset back on the phone receiver. Walks out of the telephone booth. Soon Charlie was running back down the stairs to the subway train station catching the next train to travel to the next station further up the line. Once again using the same tactics as before. Being very alert that he was not being followed. Soon, he was at his first destination and he ran upstairs Out of the tube station. He walked into a corner coffee shop. He nodded at the manager and the manager allowed him to walk through the back door of the coffee shop, just before Charlie walked through the door marked Private Charlie pointed at his mobile phone in his top breast pocket. The manager nodded slightly once more. This was a signal to make sure that the manager was switched on to keep his eyes peeled for anybody that looked out of place if they come into the coffee shop. Charlie ran down the corridors through the back private part of the Cafe shop. And back out onto the street. Then Charlie jumped into a taxi the taxi driver drove him two blocks up the road turned left then turned right Charlie paid for the taxi before the taxi stopped Then he jumped out of the taxi within the slow-moving traffic... Before long Charlie was at his destination. Charlie walked into the paper shop he could hear music playing on an MP3 player. A prearranged contact sign that it is all clear to meet his contact.

He walked up to him and just said two words. "LONDON TIMES!"

A voice replied, "Help yourself" Charlie replied, "help m.y.self?" the gentleman picked up his briefcase. And underneath it was a newspaper. Charlie placed his own paper on the table and picked up the newspaper that was underneath the gentleman's briefcase. The gentleman ignored him entirely. Charlie turned around walking briskly out of the newsagents. Then walked down the street and hailed a taxi. Soon I'm in the black taxi cab heading towards the halfway safe destination of the backdoor coffee shop. I tipped the taxi driver.

He said, "You are generous sir!" In a loud growling voice over the noise of the engine. With a slight French accent about him. Charlie stepped out of the taxi not saying a word and walked towards the back door of the coffee shop. At that moment my mobile phone rings. Charlie answer, "Yes?" The Coffee shop manager replies. "One lady and one gentleman is in the Cafe separately, Lady brown hair. In the far corner of the shop. Gentleman with a rucksack still on his back. Sitting down near the entrance."

Charlie replies, "Thanks just coming in now." Charlie puts the phone down, opens the door and walks into the corridor. Charlie grabs hold of a cup and saucer. Carried it into the coffee shop. While one of the waiters and assistant waitresses executed a diversion obscuring the vision of the two suspicious potential spies' both together the timing was excellent as the manager gave everybody the signal to obstruct. Waiting there by the door with a large wooden tray uses this to conceal Charlie, as Charlie walks into the coffee shop from the passage-Way door marked Private and he exchanges places with another gentleman at the table. And sits down at the table near to the toilet. As if he had been there all along after a visit to the men's room. He recognised the man who was sitting down at the door immediately. Not from his looks but from his body expression and personalities. He just seemed to blend in with everybody. Charlie slid his hand into his pocket and pulled out his shiny brass zippo lighter and places it on the table at an angle pointing behind him. Charlie then uses his mobile phone and sets the video recorder up and starts to film the reflection in the Zippo lighter. Of the lady sitting to the far right-hand side of him. Charlie then writes a little note on a piece of paper. And leaves it on the table next to the empty coffee cup. The word. "PTO and then Charlie wrote on the other side. PTO" then leaving this paper on the table he then stood up as usual and started to walk out of the shop. Once more pointed to his mobile phone in his top breast jacket pocket. Once again another signal to the manager. And then Charlie touched his right eye with two fingers. Another signal that there are two people in the room he has seen. The waiter replies by flicking his tea towel over his shoulder the right shoulder for yes and the left shoulder for now. The right shoulder it is. Charlie received the signal and walked out of the coffee shop. Five minutes later by this time Charlie was down in the underground and soon he receives a text message. "They looked at it." The text message was from the coffee shop manager referring to the piece of paper with PTO written on both sides. It is a little anti-surveillance trick how to confuse and confirm a spy. For a least 30 seconds. Write PTO on the both sides of the paper and the nosy spy will have to catalogue it keep turning it over please turnover, please turn over, little tricks of the trade to confirm suspicions. Charlie soon retraced his steps and he was back into his GPs practice. He opened up the newspaper and found a small post-it note with a master alarm code written on it. The system code for the Manor House has finally arrived. He opens up a programme on his office computer. And types in the code number for the alarm code into the colour blind test card system. Then Charlie photographs it on his mobile phone and then he deletes the file from the computer. And then destroys the numbers written on the post-it note he scribble over the figures first. Then placed it into the shredder. He had already had a quick check-up on the man's medical records as soon as he had found the address of the Australian gentleman, now he knows where he works what's his telephone number, etc. Charlie can now track the gentleman where he is. Knowing a person's whereabouts is a very powerful thing. Learning their movements. Covert observation surveillance using rings fencing surveillance with mobile phone technology.

Charlie downloads the photographs that he received from the lady in the coffee shop surveillance video that he had reaped from the woman in the corner of the coffee shop. Charlie uses facial recognition software and cross-references it with his medical records and the National Database and his personal records. As I say better to know your enemy.

Charlie looks up at the clock on the wall. As the minute hand strikes the door knocked. "Come in." He called out. At the same time putting his mobile phone back inside his jacket pocket. The door opened slightly to begin with. It was a young lady with her two children struggling with a pushchair at the door. So Charlie jumped up out of his chair and sprinted towards the door to hold it open for the young lady. The daughter was just standing there picking her nose while her mother was struggling with her baby brother in the pushchair. "Come in, come in please sit down."

"Oh thank you Dr I have had a terrible day."

"How can I help you, Miss Williams?"

Miss Williams was still faffing around with the pushchair and her daughter was just pain. After a few moments when the young mother had managed to settle down. Charlie sat there with the patients of an angel. Waiting for the young mother as she settles down. Finally, she managed to get both of her children under control. Dr Charlie asked once more. "How can I help you?"

The young mother said, "Well it is my leg."

The young mother starts to pull her skirt up well above the knee. Charlie averted his eyes slightly while she was making herself comfortable. Charlie noticed that she had a loose prosthetic leg. "It is the socket it is making me very sore. "Well, you have had this prosthetic leg for over a year now. And it is about time we made a new cup for you. How does that sound for you? Yes, that will be wonderful. The young girl swung her legs and kicked mother's prosthetic leg. Quite hard. The legs slid and landed on the floor. Dr said, "I am glad that was not your real one." both patient and the doctor smiled and the little girl giggled knowing full well what she had done.

"It is okay Dr she is always doing that."

Charlie does a little bit of typing on his computer and soon printed off a letter from the young mother to take to the clinic. "There you go my dear, take this to your hospital and they will help to improve things for you."

Charlie then stood up and walked towards the door and held the door open for the young mother. And soon the young mother walked out of the door and disappeared down the corridor with her wretched daughter.

Charlie closes the door and sits down in his chair. I just cannot wait till I go on this holiday, I wonder if Helen has managed to find somewhere nice and decent without going overboard. Charlie escapes for a few moments in his thoughts. And then calls the next patient in.

A mother and father walk in with their daughter concerned of their daughter's health. "Please take a seat." The mother and daughter sat down on the two chairs that were by the desk. "I'm sorry I will get your chair." I stood up and walked across the and picked up a Carver chair for the gentleman. I then sat down myself. Once everybody is comfortable Charlie asked the question. "How may I help you?" The mother looked rather worried, the mother spoke first. "It is our youngest daughter she seems to be having trouble with eating, can we have your professional opinion please Dr?" Charlie could seriously see the worry written all over the lady's face in concern of her youngest daughter.

"Yes, we can certainly have a look." Charlie looked at the little girl who was dressed lovely in a little pink flowery dress. I asked her, "That is a very nice dress you are wearing?" The little girl smiled nervously. I could sense that she was rather nervous in meeting the doctor for the first time. "So what do they call you to Young girl?"

In a very croaky voice, she answered with a great deal of pain in her face. "My name is Jade." She was even having difficulty pronouncing her own name because of the pain. She attempted to swallow after speaking her name. "My name is Charlie and it is my pleasure to meet you, I am your doctor.

I understand so! Please don't speak I know that this is quite painful for you to talk and eat." The young girl nodded. "Would you like to come over and sit on this couch, so that I can examine you?" The young girl, Jade, looked at her mother and then her father. Mother and father together said, "Yes that is okay Jade go with the very nice doctor and he will examine your throat." The young girl then turned around and looked at me. I stood up and put my hand out and offered her assistance to walk over to the couch. The couch was a little bit too hi for the young girl to sit upon it without any assistance. So I push a few buttons on the couch controller and this couch electronically slowly and steadily came down to a lower point for the young girl just to sit on it. The young girl climbed onto the couch with the assistance of her father. Now I pushed the button once more to raise the couch higher and the young girl smiled. "Good Jade now what I want to do is look inside your mouth can you open your mouth for me, please." Jade opened her mouth. And then I looked inside her mouth to see a tiny opening in the back of her throat. I also noticed that her tonsils were so far inflamed and red with an extensive amount of infection there. "Yes, I'm afraid to say that you do have tonsillitis it's pretty common for young children so there is nothing there to be worried about as it can be treated.

"I turned round to her mother and could see that she was quite relieved that it was only tonsillitis. And asked me. "Is it possible to have some antibiotics to get rid of the information," I replied, "how old is Jade?"

"Jade is three years six months old."

"Well I'm sorry to say but it's not possible to give Jade antibiotics at such a young age."

The mother instantly stepped up a gear and got rather aggressive within her body language.

And said, "I want my daughter to have antibiotics."

I replied to explain the reason why not. "There is no law against me giving your daughter antibiotics now. But your daughter is still growing, and the bacteria in your daughter's lower intestines are still developing and building up her immune system. If we interfere with this now, the bacteria in the intestines will die off. And therefore, will lower Jade's immune system considerably for the future and into her adult life. Which will then may cause her to have a problem with eczema when she is older."

The father then asked, "Dr I have my tonsils out when I was young. So is it possible to operate." His wife mumbled something, but I did not quite hear it. So I just answered the question. "There is an operation procedure brought it is not possible to operate on your daughter until she is five years old." Charlie looked at the little girl Jade, sitting on the couch. And asked her, "is it very very sore?" Little Jade nodded slowly. "Right I can give you a little bit of relief right now with some of this spray." Jade sweetly nodded again started with a smile. "Okay Jade can you open your mouth, please." Jade started to open her mouth showing her perfect pearly white teeth. I then grabbed a bottle of oral anaesthetic from out of the drawer next to the couch. "This is going to taste horrible from moment but then once that is done the pain will be gone. "Open a little wider pleases Jade." Jade opened her mouth as wide as she possibly could. So I put the nozzle of the spray into her mouth trying to avoid her tongue as much as possible. I know how horrible oral anaesthetic tastes. A quick squirt on each side of the tonsils. Jade squinted a little bit with her mouth open, as the pain must have been immense for such a small girl. Then she closed her mouth. A lovely sight of relief came over her face. "Is that better?" I asked.

A delightful smile came over Jade's face and also her mother and father as her daughter received a little bit of relief from the pain. Then jade spoke, "thank you Dr" in the lovely bright, and crisp Distinctive voice. I winked at the young girl Jade. And said, "does that feel a lot better?" Jade said, "Yes thank you." and then I began to lower the electric couch down and this time Jade giggled. "Come over and sit by your mother, Jade." Jade step down off the couch and walked briskly over to her mom and bounced up onto the seat. Jade is now pain-free and she seems to have enjoyed the experience of the examination. And the super electric flying couch. Now getting down to business. "I'm afraid that we cannot set an operation date until she is five years old. "I then started to look up the rules and regulations on the computer to try and find some way of helping this young girl without causing her problems of eczema when she's older. He looks up and finds out that there are some new products on the market especially for tonsillitis. "I'm going to prescribe you this product. It is similar to the stuff that I have just given your daughter. "It is only for pain relief and she can receive it up to 10 times a day if you can see that you need to use it more than that then bring her straight back to me. "I then handed over the prescription to the mother. I can actually see the colour coming back in her young daughter's face and she is now pain-free for the time being. "Thank you Dr and thank you for being really concerned about my daughter's' eczema from when she is older. My wife knows how serious it is as she has it," I looked over to his wife, and ask, "May I have a look?"

"Yes, doctor." And then she starts to pull her sleeve up past her elbow. From her wrist to her elbow and patches to her shoulder I can see that she was absolutely covered in aggressive excimer. "Well those look pretty aggressive to me. What sort of creams are you using?" "I am using E45 lotion and something that I pour in the bath."

"Okay, I just think that you need this one more prescription for you. Now this is in two parts the spray eases down the swelling, and the ointment to apply to four times a day and I'm sure you will see a result by the end of the week.

Then reduce application to a once-a-day treatment."

The lady's husband says, "Thank you very much Dr" "There you go, thank you very much."

"It's very nice to see you all again. And it is nice to see little Jade for the first time. So take care now." The lovely little family then happily walked out of the door. As the father was just closing the door, he showed me his thumbs up. This is one of the reasons why I love being a doctor, is to help. Two more patience of the day and then I can call it a day.

I pushed the button on my intercom. "Lilly can you send somebody in with a cup of coffee please thank you." I took my finger off the intercom and carried on typing up my report about tonsillitis.

"She said. Charlie politely replied, "Thank you, Lilly, and just put it on the desk, please." Lily place the coffee on the desk just as she was going to walk out, Charlie mentioned to Lily "this is my last practice for today and I have rather a lot of paperwork to get through so set a do not disturb on my appointments, please"

"Yes, Dr."

Then Lily turned and walked out of the room closing the door behind her.

Charlie took a nice long sip from his coffee, then stood up and walked into the little room next door to his office carrying his cup of coffee.

Charlie takes his mobile phone out of his top pocket and starts looking at the map on Google Earth zooming into the Manor house location once again studying the location on Google Earth to refresh his plan.

I am toying with the idea that he has enough time to ride over and pick up the counterfeit painting from Wolfgang and also to make the switch before the end of the day.

Charlie pulled out his burner cell phone and called Wolfgang for an arranged meeting. Charlie dials the telephone number. He places the phone to his ear and waits for the call to connect. A short pause of emptiness and the phone starts ringing soon he can hear. 3 rings pass and somebody answers the phone. "Hello who is speaking please," I replied, "cell." There was silence for a few seconds this is the response to the code. A voice stated this at the other end of the phone. "Cell is connected!" Charlie replies are we ready for a rendezvous?" The gentleman replies, "yes, but we are not quite dry yet another few minutes under the lights."

Charlie responds to the gentleman. "I will meet you at the house in 15 minutes, can you confirm this." The gentleman with a German accent replied, "yare!"

Charlie put the phone down ending the call and then opened up the phone and quickly pulled out the mobile phone chip. And pushed it into the bright yellow sharps box where all the used syringes and needles are kept after snapping it in half. He knows that this box will be destroyed by the end of the day as they are usually emptied regularly. Charlie then placed the 2nd mobile phone chip into his phone. And then turn the phone off. Charlie had called Wolfgang on the computer server telephone number. So therefore it would be untraceable. He then takes another large sip out of his coffee cup. Proceeds to get dressed out of the cabinets within the room. The last thing he grabs out of the room before he leaves. Is his rucksack? Charlie managed to sneak out as if he was a ghost quietly from the medical practice without being seen. By using the back door. He rides his motorcycle to the location, which just happens to be the Ladbrokes hotel in the centre of London right opposite the TV studios. As Charlie approaches on his bike, you could see the glorious hotel architecture. There is the main entrance under the stone archway canopy where it is very busy as people are leaving their belongings for porters to pick up. Charlie Parks his motorcycle in a side street very close to the hotel. On the right-hand side of the building, there is the sports centre doorway. Entrances to the swimming pool and the relaxation therapy room. Charlie walks straight into these rooms through and up the stairs. He walked through the higher-level corridor to one of the main maintenance lifts. And pushes the button for the top floor this list does not have any CCTV camera equipment in it. Therefore, he is free to move up the levels without being detected. The left makes its way to the top floor, as it is going up Charlie pushes the lift Bell wants and the lift carries on with his journey to the top floor. The elevators stop at the top floor and the to lift doors slide open. There is nobody there. Charlie waits for a moment. And suddenly a gentleman walks around the corner and straight into the lift. Charlie ignores him. And also the gentleman ignores Charlie. The gentleman pushes the next floor down on the lift buttons. The doors close and the lift and starts to move. "Hello, Charlie." The gentleman said. "Hello Wolfgang," Charlie replied. "Nice to meet you again Wolfgang, do you have it." "Yes." And Wolfgang starts to pull out a long cylinder from the sleeve of his jacket. And Charlie also pulls out a brown envelope full of cash and the exchange is made. "Till next time then,"

"Yes it's my pleasure, Wolfgang." The lift bounces as it comes to a stop the lift doors open on and Wolfgang walks out of the lift. Charlie pushes the next button down to the lower levels as he steps out he pushes the button in the lift one floor down from the top floor sending the elevator back up to Wolfgang. And then I retrace my steps out of the main building through the quiet leisure centre within the hotel complex and out of the door onto the main street into the noisy traffic and busy footpaths. Charlie blended in with the pedestrians smoothly and headed towards his motorcycle.

Soon Charlie is back on his motorcycle heading on his way towards the Manor house.

CHAPTER 8

"Hello Glenn, it's a weak signal you will have to speak up. I cannot actually hear you clear enough. Are you on your way? Or are you in Telford?" Glenn replies over the breaking up digital phone signal. "I'* *n *elfo**." Charlie Can also slightly here an electric roller shutter door motor noise in the background while Glenn was speaking. Milliseconds before the phone signal disconnected. Charlie wasn't sure whether he was in Telford or on his way. All I can do is to deduce from what he said that he would be visiting over soon one day this week. Never mind, it will all work out. I will just wait for a better reception before I call him again. Charlie's mobile phone Vibrated unexpectedly in his jacket pocket making the alarm sound of an old car horn for a minute or 2. Charlie did not hear it over the sound of his motorcycle or even feel the vibrations from his phone, Charlie carried on with his secret mission unchanged.

Manoeuvring through the backcountry roads on the way towards market Drayton, and the Manor house. Charlie knows he only sustained a small time envelope and he must make this deadline. So Charlie is actually cutting a groove and pins the throttle of his motorcycle at every opportunity. The white lines in the road were flying by. He is keeping his vision as far ahead as possible, knowing full well his bike will go where ever he looks at these speeds they will be getting there fast so he traces the road with his eyes exactly where he wants to go in advance of himself.

A sign flies past him. A quick glance from Charlie revealed that it said, "10 miles to market Drayton." Today he is really gunning for it. Hugging the fuel tank to his legs and chest, also on his toes keeping the pressure along the foot pegs as he is at full tilt he dares not look at his Speedo for a moment from the fear of losing the fine line of concentration. So I cannot tell you how fast Charlie is moving up the road but suddenly Charlie prepares himself for the bends ahead of him and he is leaning over as far as he possibly can be on his knee. As he duzz His knee is scraping the tarmac as he takes the right-hand bend. The plastic slider on his knee protected him and is saving his knee from destruction. Then the roads straightened up and Charlie continue to read the road perfectly following the contours of the road ahead twist and turns of the twisty road as if he was on the TT.

A humpback bridge sign came up along the road. I know I only have 50 m to break at the speed I don't know if I'm starting to make it, I banged it down through the gears and use my front brake. The bike slows down rapidly but is it enough. Suddenly I hit the bridge the bike is airborne I still retain the same position on my bike just grip my knees a little bit harder to take the pressure off the foot pegs as I hit the bridge I ride that bike like a jockey. While I am airborne, I think of nothing else but keeping my eyes on the road my mind makes the natural calculations for me at these speeds it is too fast to think. You think of these speeds and change your judgement for a 2nd you are dead. But this was not the case at this moment as I hold my concentration at all times and never ever take my eyes off the track that I am riding on this road. I came across this skill many years ago on my pushbike as a young boy and have never forgotten it since. When I used to hold onto the lorries and get towed at high speeds down jiggers bank. Jump the humps while overtaking the lorry on my pushbike taking the bend at the bottom at high speed at approximately 50 miles an hour. Flying past the little corner shop on the Bend and passed the 2 pubs each side of the road this was well before the traffic lights had ever been installed.

5 miles past like a breeze. Time to slow it down. The turning is here someplace. A staggered junction sign is hidden halfway into the hedgerow. All I see is a red part of a triangle. I know this means a T-junction or a give-way sign or even a slow bend. Don't ever risk it, just slow down, and keep your buffers large. Soon into the speed limit and down through the gears. It was the sign of the junction a quick lifesaver manoeuvre indicates check the mirrors and around the bend I go. Somewhere around here the dirt track that leads to the rear of the Manor House. I must not take my motorcycle to close. So I find a decent place to park my bike out of view. There is a field gate. A quick look around and there is nobody near. Charlie is at a total stop. He put the bike on its side stand and dismounted the bike. On approaching the gate. "Dammit, there is a good Yale padlock." Charlie did not worry about this; he picked that padlock as if he had the keys in his hand. Quickly he has simply and easily opened the gate and rolled his BMW motorcycle into the field behind the hedge. Closing the gates

behind him then proceeded to camouflage it with sticks and any branches and long grass that he could find close to hand.

Making sure everything was in his rucksack that he was prepared for. Including the very notions of the painting. A quick look at the compass. To get my bearings, I look through the slit after orientating the compass with a large tree and orienteering map in the far distance. So I bounded on my bearing in that direction skirting around the outside of the field, keeping myself low not to give away my position, it did not take me long to get to the tree plotting the reference points. So I looked back and orientated myself back to my motorcycle. This is my waypoint. So I wrote my 5-figure grid reference down on a piece of paper of my motorcycles-location. If I have to bug out, I'm going to have to find this fast. So I also memorise any landmarks to make sure that I am fully orientated to my environment. As I am in the field as I start stalking. I'm sure your buddies out there have been in that similar sort of situation before; as you are conditioned for this it's the job. This is what I miss so much the thrill the excitement the planet and expertise to the highest skill set. All the orientation is complete and now it's time to get on and makeup sometime. The Manor house is not in view, however. It's a good 2 miles away as the crow flies 10 minutes running time. There are many fields I have to cross and I cannot just go straight to the house for fear of leaving any tracks. Stealth is the key.

10 minutes literally have passed and the house is in sight. A quick check up on the Google Earth photograph that I had printed off earlier that day to verify location.

Yes, all is correct. Suddenly a farm tractor is heard starting up in the distance close to the direction of the Manor house, so I keep myself Low to avoid Silhouette in myself on the horizon above hedgerow or even climbing over a gate. I must get in and out without being seen noticed or recognised. A dog barks in the distance as the farm tractor pulls onto the courtyard. Being fully aware of the dog at this time, the fear of this animal giving away my position. Soon, I am across the tarmac strip of road. Ducking down behind a dry stonewall quietly finding good cover. Where I can survey and find my route in. There is the three-storey manor house. Yes, I can get to it through the backfield luckily all the cattle are out of the fields in the milking parlour. So there is a lot of noise going on in the local farmyard. Now my chance I'm sliding over the fence with as little profile manageable I pulled my rucksack through the gate on my drag bag line. After a short run in the Manor House garden. I can hear children playing somewhere close. It was a large Tudor house with 3 stories and 4 rows of sash windows and the larger door to the side. All the windows were covered in newspaper. I thought that was quite unusual. But then I remember my wife had said that he has only just moved into the Manor house a quick recce ran to the side door. I pulled out my lock picking tools. And approached the door crouching down as low as possible I listened to doorframe moment with a stethoscope against the side door and the earpieces in my ear. The manor house was silent. I pulled my silicone latex gloves on. I'm all dressed in black with a balaclava on so why should be quite difficult to see in the shadows of the doorway. These old farmhouse locks are a cinch. And soon the door swings open. I pulled out my mat and rolled it out inside the hallway. I stepped onto the mat and closed the door quietly behind.

As soon as the door is shut I quickly pulled on my leather overshoes. Fast running as stealthily as I probably could towards the main alarm box on the wall at the end of the corridor near the main door.

I found it.

I flipped down the plastic cover and started punching the code. "Beep!" The alarm is disabled. Now I have to go and have a search for this precious painting, the card players. It's upstairs I know my wife told me. The 1st floor here we go. Just down the corridor I walked. Turned left there were the stairs.

I walked up them, up the side of the stair treads holding onto the banister rail making sure that I slowly walked up the stairs by putting my body weight pressure on each foot steadily, as I creep silently up the stairs. Everywhere I looked in the house, it's looking like it's in the middle of refurbishment and DIY decorating. Soon I am nosing through the upper-level corridor. Write I know it is in one of these rooms, my wife said there was a lovely view of the farmhouse. That's the room where the painting was last identified.

So this is the far corner Charlie needs to check 1st. listening carefully and moving steadily Charlie swiftly move down the corridor. At the end of the dusty second-floor hall. The last closed door on the left of the bare oak full-boarded corridor. The door was locked, but somebody had left the key in the keyhole, so a smooth, steady, turn, of the old cast-iron key. Soon the door is unlocked revealing the secrets as easy as that. Quietly pushing the heavy oak door open steadily while kneeling down on one knee. Soon in

Charlie went. But 1st he, thoughtfully placed another set of new overshoes over his first set of overshoes to prevent dirty footprints from the dusty oak wooden hallway. As He stepped over the threshold onto the clean newly Briar waxed ring, oak boarded floor, Charlie walked entering this clean Aladdin's Cave of fine art and household artefacts of what seemed to be an avid collector of precious antiquities. Of the only door, that was closed and locked. It looks like a treasure room. Amazingly it seemed as though the entire household wealth has been collected into this place for safe keeping, Away from decorators and their dust and prying eyes.

Resembling a very exclusive car boot sale. There are no paintings hanging on the walls in the room that had been stripped bare sanded and filled.

Not that I expected this but all the paintings were stacked neatly in order on tables and chairs.

As it was evident there, they were in the midst of decorating.

Charlie searched through and looked at several paintings and could not find it. Then Charlie turned around and walked towards the door and he spotted a glimpse of another old gilt picture frame under a white towel. Carefully Charlie peeled off the white Bath towel. Oh, my! There it is, as Charlie takes a deep breath in With his eyes wide open he is staring at. One of the excellent vintage paintings by Paul Cézanne of the card players worthy of £250 million sterling. This is one of 5 paintings in his series and this was one of his last portraits ever. The crown jewel of artists. The most sought after and valuable art in the world to date, so I checked this rapidly, for authenticity to my amazement it is original. I wasted no time in taking this, and pulling out my cylinder containing Wolfgang's counterfeit painting out of my rucksack and proceeded to unroll this counterfeit canvas out on the table in front of him. Charlie compared the 2 fine art masterpieces these paintings together side-by-side. The counterfeit painting was not noticeably a shade lighter in a few colours. "Wolfgang you are a gifted artist of counterfeits fine arts masters." While this painting is Next to the original Master. I could hear children playing outside not screaming just singing nursery rhymes playing happily altogether, it was quite eerie but at the same time very soothing to the soul. Soon I had the counterfeit painting in its frame and began rolling up the original Fine Art painting in between my protective leather pigskin mat to conserve the delicate art of the card players and carefully placing this 17th-century gem into its protective tube.

With the original fine arts master painting in his rucksack on his back, Charlie walked across the room and put the counterfeit art back on the chair in the exact place as shown from the imprints on top of the leather seat. Charlie immediately re-covered it with the white towel once more. Charlie could hear the children singing outside in the farm Courtyard "Ringa, Ringa roses a pocket full of poses." As he walked out of the room into the corridor locking the oak door behind him and leaving the key back in the same position in the keyhole. The window at the end of the hallway was also covered in the newspaper except one of the corners that have been ripped off the window. As he took a few steps towards the window but still approximately 6 feet away from the window to avoid any light casting onto his face, either giving away his location or identification. All it takes is one of the children to say that they seen a man's face in the window, I am sure I do not have to point out the consequences if this had happened. Charlie could oversee the farm Courtyard and the children cheerfully enjoying themselves singing out loud.

5 little girls all dressed up so cute. This just made me think a little bit of what I was doing with my life. Not with stealing this painting, but thinking about my lovely wife wanting a baby. At that moment, I felt quite safe and secure in this house. The children looked so happy. And it just gave me one of those beautiful feelings that you feel. I just suppose I was feeling my body clock ticking thinking that it was the right time for a child.

So I pulled out my mobile phone from my inside pocket and turned it on. I know what you are thinking what a silly move that is giving my GPS location away on my mobile phone instantly. But now I'm deeply in love and I want to speak to my wife and tell her how much I love her and that I agree that we will try for a baby together. The phone rings. The children are still singing round in a circle. As I can see them out of the window. Then suddenly I can hear a mobile phone ringing. I dropped down to my knees as quick as lightning. I swear there was nobody in the house. The phone still rings and keeps on ringing. It is the exact same ringtone as my wife's mobile and it's coming from that room. So I walked across the corridor in a stealthy manoeuvre as low as I possibly could and close to the wall. The door was wide open and I looked around the base of the doorjamb straight into a beautiful white bedroom. With a large four-poster bed in it, so I walked into the room and the bed was a mess, but there was nobody in theirs. The phone stopped ringing, but it was definitely somewhere in this room. So I walked in further after looking around the room I notice my wife's painting on the wall pride of place of the waterfall on the

139

chimney breast. My heart is heavy and I feel quite sick and annoyed as I can see also what looked like the bin bags that I had only loaded in my wife's car that very morning. But there were only 2 bags instead of 4. And no boxes. So I pushed my fingers into the plastic bags and ripped them open and realise that Those Clothes in there could have been my wives. But I did not recognise them I was still sick. Charlie carried on to looking for this mobile phone it was on the floor underneath the bed. So Charlie kneels down he was genuinely hoping that it was not her phone and picked up this mobile phone and checked for the missed call up on it. Yes, oh fu*k. As Charlie positively identifies the phone. How could she do this to me? It was definitely my wife's phone because I was the last person to phone her just only 1 minute ago. There on the screensaver was a photograph of me carrying that very nice bottle of wine in the oak casket, that day we celebrated her art exhibition. I should have left this phone exactly where it lay. But he didn't he put it safely away into his jacket pocket. Right, that woman is out of my life. But I must play it cautiously. And make sure everything is correct before I terminate the relationship. Charlie could feel such intense anger and hurt this is virtually immobilising him. Right, I have to get going out of this house.

I cannot stand it any longer thinking that my wife had been having sex on that antique oak four poster king size double bed. I made sure everything was back to normal and back in its place. The only thing that I could not fix was the bin bag that I have ripped open with my fingers. I did my best, though, to make sure that it was not seen so easily.

Come on Charlie time to get out of here! Giving myself some encouragement to move, move! Move! Move! My inner voice screamed out to me! God dammit she might as well of just stabbed me in my heart.

Move! Move! Move! My inner voice said again. So I stepped backwards a couple of steps and then turned around and walked out of the room and down the corridor to the main stairs I walked down the stairs normally steadily and quietly close to the banister rail holding my weight and spreading my weight evenly over the 2 steps as I walked down the stairs.

Deep inside me it was boiling up. Gotta stay professional got to do my job. My inner voice cried out to me. At the bottom of the stairs, I turned and ran down the Minton tiled ground floor corridor.

Towards the same door that Charlie earlier entered in with. Dammit, the alarm I must reset the alarm. My mind is all over the place must concentrate. My inner voices are telling me all sorts of things all different scenarios are running through my mind. Whose was the 2nd blindfold that was in that dusty pink bag? Just the other week. "Feck it, Feck it." The alarm which is the code number. I punched in what I thought was the code number to reset the alarm and to delete the last alarm time setting. (Beep) The alarm is set and I just ran down the corridor to the door I opened the door not really looking out through the door, which was another one of my mistakes. I went to close the door. Behind me. But then I remembered my mat. I knelt down reaching in into the doorway and pulling out my mat. Locking the door behind me and running for cover when I should have crawled away from the door. Retracing my steps back not bothering much about my footprints this time.

But making my way out of the garden over the backyard fence into the allotment and just jumped over the 5 bar gate and ran across the road. Just as the tractor was driving out of the other farm entrance about 20 feet down the road. I dived into the hedge over the other side of the road. The tractor driver must have seen me as the tractor driver drove past my location as I crawled through the bottom of the hedge. As quick as I could. Even though it was a major struggle fighting through the hedge as my rucksack got snag up in the hedgerow and one of my latex gloves got ripped off my hand. As I was battling and struggling through the hedge, I was getting so annoyed with myself. As the tractor was driving, past me, I was definitely not concentrating. I waited for that tractor to drive past me totally as I am in deep cover under the hedge before I made my move. While I was waiting for the tractor to pass I gathered up the ripped silicon glove and stuffed it in my pocket, I could smell the earthy rotting leaves underneath the hedgerow in the mossy high grass bank. Soon Charlie Slowly crawled into the field and then ran as fast as he could along the hedgerow. By now the adrenaline is pumping through my veins. This powerful drug in my body makes me move faster and faster. Charlie jumps over the next 5 bar gate. And carried on running. By this time the tractor had entered one of the fields and was heading towards my location at speed. Field after field I ran.

Until I could see the tree of my waypoints grid on the horizon. Come on not much further. One more fence. Charlie jumped over this razor wire fence and suddenly slipping on a mossy sandstone boulder beneath the fence losing his foothold. Razor wire fence catching and cutting into his arm on it ripping deep into Charlie's arm and shirt, cutting myself severely it was quite deep from the razor wire fence I was bleeding leaving evidence of my DNA at the scene. The tractor is speeding closer come on go-go-go. Soon I was back with my motorbike. And the tractor was going through the gate in the bottom field. I'm under pressure to get the gate open as fast as I can and also take the camouflage off my bike and soon pushing it out of the field also closing the gate behind me. As I jumped up on it and pushed the electric start. The bike burst into life, I have shifted it into gear and I am just releasing the clutch and up comes the front wheel as I wheelie off down the road seriously, I did not mean to wheelie this motorbike down the road behind the high hedges. Got to get home this is going to be the fastest 30 miles I've ridden.

As I am riding as fast as I can. I'm not really concentrating on the road as my thoughts are elsewhere. I noticed a few minor incidents close calls and near misses it showing me that I am not concentrating sufficiently enough at this speed.

But for some reason I know that I have to get home as soon as possible, and now it is just race against the clock.

Soon the turn comes up to head into Newport. Charlie will take this turning into Newport, as it is a lot faster than going around the bypass also avoiding the police speed trap near the bypass island, into the Newport town I go. I stopped at the island because there was a massive lorry turning. I look to the right-hand side of myself reflected in the library window. My reflection was crystal clear and God did I look good on my bike with my specially adapted all black leather and canvas motorcycle gear.

The lorries' wheels were scrubbing on the tarmac as it turned its tight turning around the island. This was a Left-hand drive lorry and this truck was showing foreign number plates. There is no reason why a large truck like that should be in Newport high Street. The international lorry driver must have gotten lost. Soon there was enough clearance behind the lorry for me to ride my motorcycle through the high Street, so I took my opportunity and went for it. SOD the 20-mile an hour speed limit and I gunned it through the village at 30 miles an hour, thankfully I wasn't seen by the local constabulary. Sharply turning right at the Shakespeare pub to exit Newport high Street carrying on past the local police station pinning it from the outer limits of the town to the New Ireland. The island is clear so Charlie carried on around seamlessly with his knee down as he powered up on the throttle as he came out smoothly from the turn from the island. Pinned it again straight down the bypass to the next island around the island again with his knee down straight over this time. Then pinning it again, down the bypass smoothly slipping up through his gears. 2nd, 3rd, 4th, 5th, 6th, power wheeling up slightly on each gear change. Straight down the straight road, down the middle of the traffic. Cars just seemed like there was standing still as Charlie flew down the long straight cautiously taking the bend as there is a staggered junction then dropping it down one gear and pinning the throttle once more a quick glimpse at my Speedo I can see that I'm doing 160 miles an hour. And still he is keeping the throttle pinned he can start to feel the wind vibrations getting more violent on his helmet as he is approaching the top speed of the motorcycle 200 miles an hour plus.

The farmers' service Bridge is in sight, and 150 m behind this bridge is an island, so it is off the throttle a little bit rapid and down through the gears as I approach the bridge. Then slowing down to a moderate pace as I approach the clock island. I came to a dead stop, as the island was pretty busy. Luckily I did this, as at the moment a large military tank came whizzing round the bend and around the island. Those 2 Rolls-Royce V8 engines powering this mighty military hardware around the island I gave the co-pilot a nod and he replied with a nod. I smiled, as I think he may also be a motorcyclist. A blip of the throttle also indicating that I'm going to head straight over the island. Soon I'm at the other side of the island passing Macdonald on the left hand side opening up the throttle, stepping through my gears the back wheel squirms a little bit. I must have hit a patch of diesel oil on the road. Fast approaching the next island the way is clear so I took the island around it approximately 50 miles an hour in 2nd gear and then came out of the island and pinned it at the other side of the island cutting grooves down the road as I am riding my motorcycle as if I have stolen it. The next island approaches, after a long straight bend, onto the island's straight round with my knee down and straight into the industrial estate riding my motorcycle like a legend. After 5 more minutes of riding flat out I approach my house. My BMW RRS 1000 has done me proud. 15 minutes in total from the Manor house in market Drayton now that is a new record for me. I cruised the motorcycle slowly up the drive at the 1st glance everything looked as it normally does. My wife's car was not there as I expected it. Apparently she has already left. I feel this sick feeling coming over me once more, so that moment I parked my motorcycle outside of the garage. Kicking down the bike rest. Dismounting I pushed the button on the motorcycle handlebars to open the double garage doors. The roller doors started to come up as the garage doors rolled up I still have this unbelievable feeling within me that I could not shake off anger and aggression was coursing through my veins along with the adrenaline of the awesome motorcycle ride that I have just performed. I turned to take my rucksack off at the same time looking into the garage allowing my eyes to get accustomed to the low light in the garage.

To my horror, I can see Glenn slumped against the wall in a pool of blood at the back of the garage. As I ran forward to him, he held his hand up to me. And then he pointed over to the right-hand side of him, there was a body lying on the floor lifeless holding a knife in his hand. I immediately ran over to the man lying on the ground with a dagger loosely gripped in his hand. I dived onto his back to disarm him immediately. And put my foot on the back of his hand to hold him down but there was no movement from this man. No gust of air out of his mouth as I landed on his back. So I pulled the bloody knife out of this dead man's fingers. Then I checked his pulse on his neck with my 2 fingers there was nothing there I could not detect apples so from my medical experiences I can deduce that this man is dead. I dropped the bloody dagger on the floor as I looked over to Glenn he was struggling to breathe as he was holding the most up part of his ribs on the side of his chest. I quickly moved forward to Glenn's position as he was sitting up against the back garage wall. 5 feet away from the body. "Don't say anything Glenn,"

"He flocking jumped me – a cough-cough,"

"It is all safe now Glenn,"

"Don't say anything Glenn just stay there I'm going to put you in a prone position so you can reflate your lungs,"

Charlie proceeded to move Glenn into a recovery position more comfortable on the garage floor. This only took a moment. And then he stood up and pushed the garage door closing mechanism on the wall. The shutter came down in a garage room was engulfed in darkness. Charlie flicked the switch for the fluorescent lights. Blink-blink crackle-crackle as the lights flickered and burst into life flooding the garage with bright fluorescent light.

"Glenn is you all right?"

"Yes, I am cold, though." Quietly he said this was lying on the floor in the prone position. Charlie checks his pulse. His pulse was very erratic but strong. He was showing early signs of shock. So I pulled off my motorcycle helmet and placed it on the floor And then my motorcycle jacket to cover Glenn.

"I must get some dressings on this for you. You must wait there for a moment Glenn tries not to move. I'm going to get my first aid box. Immediately Charlie walked off and out the garage door straight into the house through the adjoining door still my wife was not home.

Charlie looked underneath the kitchen sink for the first aid box. He grabbed this as fast as he could and also a handful of sugar lumps from the kitchen island and turned back around and ran back into the garage. The bleeding had from Glenn had subsided quite drastically now I have put some pressure on the damaged area. I don't know how deep the stab wound is, but I know that no major organs have been damaged. Although there are a lot of blood vessels around that area. "Come on Glenn stay with us now don't close your eyes keep looking at me, Charlie then pushed a sugar lump into Glenn's mouth to try and reverse the effects of shock. Charlie said to Glenn, "I've got to pick your shirt up to assess the damage is that okay? Glenn replied, "Yes-yes". There was a little three-quarter of an inch approximately 15 mm cut in Glenn's side. Luckily enough the knife had gone into and through his wallet 1st. I looked over at the knife and I could determine the width of the blade to the depth of the penetrating stab wound. Charlie rapidly worked on Glenn by putting a bandage and field dressing over the injured area. "Is that more comfortable for you Glenn."

"Absolutely Charlie you have saved my life."

"No Glenn it looks like that you have saved my life." Glenn struggled a little bit in pain. But managed to speak. "He was waiting for you in the garage."

"Who the hell is he?"

"I have no idea, but I know he just stabbed me by surprise as I was going to get into the car."

"Right let's have a look at this mongrel." Charlie stood up and walked over to the gentleman lying there on the floor facedown. He then got hold of the man's hair and pulled his head back as far as he dares to have a look at the man's face. To his disbelief, he recognised him straight away. "God dammit I don't believe it, it's the Australian gentleman from the art exhibition he bought my wife's painting, "Oh sh*t, I hope she's already cashed the cheque?" and from that day I thought that I was catching the glimpse of him in the crowds. You know a funny feeling you feel like you are being followed. "Yes I know exactly what you mean," a heavy breathe out from Glenn. "So what the hell are we going to do then." as Charlie slowly puts the face of this man back down onto the concrete

"I don't know we are just going to have to think about it, but this body cannot stay here in the open." Disposing of a body or concealing the body is against the law and it is a jailing offence.

"Yes, but I believe that this bastard has had an affair with my wife."

"Flock need Charlie how the hell did that happen and how did you find out."

"It's a long story it's too early to tell you now."

"We have got to get rid of this body where we going to put it."

Charlie rubs his hand through his hair as the stress was taking hold as Charlie was thinking it through.

"Charlie! You are bleeding too." I don't worry about that I scratch myself on some barbed wire." Charlie describes out some disinfectant spray out of his first aid box. And sprays it onto the cut." it stung quite a lot but Charlie just gritted his teeth and carried on.

"What do you suggest we should do Glenn?"

"How the hell should I know I couldn't think straight? All I know is we have got to get this body out of here. "Charlie paced up and down the garage just trying to think clearly.

"How are you feeling me Glenn can you stand up?"

"All I will do my best to which you are going to have to help me." Charlie reached out towards Glenn, "give me your hand." Glenn placed his hand into Charlie's hand and made attempts to stand up. After a peaceful struggle of getting his balance and also feeling rather weak from the blood, loss, Glenn managed to get up onto his feet. Now he's standing leaning up against the car. Charlie said, "don't let your blood get on my car." Charlie checked Glenn's pulse once more and notice that his pulse and evened out and was steady. "How is your breathing Glenn?"

"It's not so bad now I can feel that both lungs are working."

"Glenn you had a very lucky escape there if your wallet had not saved you from being stabbed."

"I know, I know I cannot bear thinking about it. It just happened so fast you must have sneaked in underneath the shutter door as I was closing the door I noticed a reflection in the car window I just thought it was you, Charlie. And then I have seen his arm, around so I ducked and as I did he stabbed me I managed to get behind him and get my arm around his neck and did not let loose until he fell on the floor. And that's where they lay."

"Why the flock was he in here, apparently he thought you were me? Well, we do look alike don't with Glenn well I suppose?"

"Will you suppose we have the similar hair colour and we are similar height also even though I am a lot shorter than you?"

"Charlie, do you think there is a hit out on you?"

"They could very well be Glenn. At least I know it's not you."

"You suck we are best buddies."

"Just making it clear that I trust you."

"Glenn replies, "of course I know that we have been through it together!"

"Anyway, we have got no time to waste should take your jacket and shirt off and your trousers. I will go upstairs and get you some fresh clothes. You stop in the garage because nobody has seen you yet."

Charlie made his way out of the garage up the stairs inside the house and started looking for clothes for Glenn. Was Glenn is in the garage getting undressed.

Charlie is soon back into the garage with a bin bag and some rubber gloves and the role of Clingfilm. Also some various rags and cleaning chemicals and a bottle of salt. "I will clean this up you wrapped this around you waste 1st before you get dressed." Charlie started mopping up the blood on the floor with Glenn's old clothes and pouring salt into the blood. He then threw the dirty, bloody rags into the large bin bag carried on doing this until all the blood had gone. Now to kill the D.N.A Charlie poured bleach onto the floor and also some hospital blood cleaning fluid. Glenn was struggling with putting one of Charlie's shirts on, Charlie pulled off on, and Charlie pulled off his silicon rubber gloves and pushes them into the bin bag along with the bloody clothes. And then gave Glenn a little hand to finish getting dressed. "It looks like that dressing is holding well Glenn?"

"Yes Charlie it is, and I do believe it has stopped bleeding,"

"No Glenn it has not had time to heal I'm going to have to give you a few stitches, but we will do that later. Let's sort this out 1st."

"Okay, Charlie."

Tomlin grabbed hold of the large bin bag full of bloody clothes. "Give me a moment I'm going to destroy these in the barbecue." Charlie walked towards the garage door leading into the house. Passing the bench he grabbed hold of a large bottle of liquid fire lighter and walked out of the door. Glenn just stood in the garage fumbling around for his cigarettes and then realised Charlie was just going to burn them. "Oh fu*k it there in my jacket, bollocks! I suppose now is the time to think about giving up." Glenn was really Pis*ed off now because he really did need a cigarette.

Just only a couple of minutes later Charlie walked back into the garage through the door. The golden glow of flames was reflecting on the door as the barbecue was roaring. Charlie joked, "Fancy a few stakes, Glenn, as Charlie looked down at the body on the floor."

"You are flocking idiot, we would never be able to eat him all in one day have you seen the size of him?"

"You are one sick mother Fokker."

Anyway: let's get going.

Charlie says, "It looks like you could do with a cigarette Glenn."

Charlie throws Glenn his wallet with a big stab knife mark through the centre of it.

Glenn catches it in his one hand. "Did you get my cigarettes, Charlie?"

"What cigarettes?"

"The cigarettes in my trouser pocket you Dumbo,"

Charlie smiled, "I suppose you deserve a cigarette," and Charlie threw him a packet of 20, over towards him.

"Thank you, Charlie. You are a lifesaver."

"Yeah-yeah-yeah-yeah. You enjoy your cigarette I will have a look at this idiot on the floor."

Charlie started searching through his pockets there was nothing in his pockets except one bunch of keys. " Glenn I have found some keys in his pocket there must be a vehicle somewhere here did you notice any cars parked at the side of the road when you came in," "no I didn't."

Charlie asks himself this question. Now where would I park my car? The only place that I know what is a straight road and on turning off we will just have to go back and have a look. Charlie then puts the car keys into his pocket. And then he carries on searching the Australian man's pockets a mobile phone ton puts this in his pocket as well. Nothing else in his pockets. The man was wearing black denim jeans and a dark green jacket with an old farmer peaked cap. Charlie automatically thinks that he has done his recce quite well. And the juices that this man is a professional as he has done his field craft by blending into the environment and to the local clothing fashion.

"Glenn, do you think that you are capable of driving?"

"Yes, no problem."

"But this is how we are going to have to go about it, we put the body on the back seat of the Mercedes on top of some bin bags. I will drive and you can keep your head down in the passenger seat. We will go out and find his car and then you will drive his car somewhere else. And I will dispose of the body."

"Yes, Charlie good plan let's gets going."

Charlie pulls out a black tarpaulin from off-the-shelf. And starts to spread it out over the back seats. Then picks the body up onto his feet and then lifted him up onto his shoulders and then carried him around the car and struggled to push him in the back door on the Mercedes. The dead body is now loaded into the car. And Charlie pulls the tarpaulin over the top of the body to conceal him."

"On Glenn get in the Charlie opens up the car on me and Glenn get in the car. "Charlie opens up the on Glenn get in the car." Charlie opens up the garage door as Glenn is lying down in the passenger seat. The roller shutter doors open smoothly and Charlie walks outside and starts his motorbike up. And drives it into the garage and parks it up. Turning off the engine and jumping off the bike, Charlie was soon back into the Mercedes-Benz in the driver's seat. He drove out the garage as normal. And close the garage door behind him. "Glenn which side of the road did you comin on?"

"I came in from the right." "Okay, so we will go left there is a good place down here to hide a car. A lot of public walk their dogs around here."

Thank God there is a key fob on the key ring. Glenn asks, "What colour are we looking for?"

"Well it is a Skoda key ring, so we will start looking for Skoda's it comes to the layby." Keep your head down. Slowly does it, Charlie drives past a pretty miserable looking Skoda car. Type of car that your granddad would push Glenn."

Charlie pushes the key fob. "Clicked" yes that's the one" As the hazard lights flash. "Are you going to be all right to walk Glenn?"

"Yes, that don't make it too far while there are no cars around here at the moment and I cannot see anybody walking."

Charlie replies, "Yes I do agree with Glenn you can just jump out now, here is the keys take them get the car started and drive to Birmingham."

Drop the car on the outskirts I will follow you and we will drop the car off at a local dogging site, you know that place you showed me many years ago," "yes okay," okay all clear go-go-go. Glenn jumped out of the car walked over to the Skoda. He pulled the door handle and the locks had been opened Glenn and had pulled on a pair of leather gloves that Charlie had given him. Sitting down in the driver's seat Glenn made sure that he did not move the seating position or any other controls. Charlie drove off and waited just around the corner. It wasn't long before Glenn was behind Charlie. And sooner were driving to their prearranged destination towards the M54, Junction near Shifnal. Charlie looked in his rear-view mirror Glenn looked perfect. A good distance behind driving as the grey man wearing a flat cap. Soon we were that the island and the traffic lights we just on Amber I made a signal to Glenn with my hand for him to stop at the traffic lights as I went through Glenn listened and stopped at the lights. The road was clear at all the island injunctions and also the slip road onto the main Motorway. I drove down three-quarters of the way down the slip road, I stopped and jumped out of the car there is no time to lose I quickly opened the back seat door and pulled the body out, throwing him over my shoulder and running as fast as I can into the woods there was a branch. On the floor and I lies the body up. So that the branch would hit this man in the throat as if he had fallen over and placed his hands into the position that he would have put his hands forward to break his fall. Then I ran back to the waiting car jumped into the driver's seat and started to drive off. Soon I noticed the old man's Skoda coming down the slippery as a sequence of the traffic lights must have just completed their change. Glenn followed me to the next location to drop off the car. I noticed the car was occasionally weaving on the motorway and I thought that Glenn could be getting quite seriously ill with internal bleeding. It was not long before we were as there at the location even though it felt like an age. I gave Glenn the thumbs down to park the car. Glenn popped up. I drove just a little bit down the road and then turns around and drove back past Glenn walking in the direction where he just came from. I slowed down considerably and Glenn Cross the road and jumped into the rear passenger seat and slump down to hide his presence on the backseat. Charlie continued to drive back home but through a different route this time avoiding the motorway, as there are road cameras on the motorway there are no cameras on the slip road not at Shifnal for anyway.

Half an hour later Glenn and Charlie were back at the house, after parking the car in the garage.

"Come on Glenn let's get you fixed up and have a look at this wound."

Glenn lifted up his shirt. To reveal a blood-soaked field dressing. They both know from training that a field dressing only holds one point of blood. So you can work out how fast the person is bleeding and keep account of the amount of field dressings you use. A matter-of-fact, if you use more than 6 you are extremely critical. And if you use 8. Then you are saying your prayers.

Charlie put his arm around Glenn and gives him a hand out into the garden and down into the wine cellar. "Come on Glenn let me give you a hand onto the table." Charlie struggled to get Glenn up onto the table. As by now he was starting to feel quite a bit week. Charlie pulls out his doctor's bag. And then begins to prepare Glenn. Charlie has everything that needs to complete this operation. All of the surgical and sterilised equipment that you would find in any normal operating theatre. Charlie had also rescued an operating theatre light and had it installed inside his wine cellar. You never know when you are going to need an emergency operating theatre. "Are you comfortable Glenn?" Yes, I am."

"I'm going to give you some gas breathe it in nice and deep but don't hold your breath." Glenn Holt's mask over his face and started breathing in the gas and air. It can feel giggly feeling coming over him. Knowing full well it is working now. "Are you feeling lightheaded yet Glenn?'

"Yes, go-ahead Charlie."

"Okay making my 1st incision now."

For god's sake, Charlie don't tell me what you are doing it bad enough as it is just operate on me."

"Sorry, Glenn force of habit." Charlie starts putting into the flesh of Glenn. He needs to explore and get enough room to sew the wound from the inside out. Charlie finds out that is a lot more dangerous than his 1st thought. Charlie rolls out his surgical tools and finds the leaky blood vessel and prints it inside of the cut. Thankfully this blood vessel is not cut all the way through. So Charlie proceeds to sew him up. The blood vessels are sewn up even though it was quite finicky small and challenging. Charlie carries on sewing stitches after stitching with dissolvable stitches. That's it the muscle is completely sewn up now. Charlie has a quick look at Glenn his breathing steadily. But his eyes are closed and he is gritting his teeth. In silence, Charlie carries on working on him at least 2 hours have passed and Charlie is putting in the final stitches to close his good friend up. Charlie pulls away the gas and air from Glenn. And checks his pulse. Glenn opened one eye and he looked thoroughly stoned. "All finished now Glenn." there was no reply from Glenn except a small nod of the head. Charlie sat down on the chair next to Glenn and nursed him for about an hour. Waiting for Glenn to come around out of his operation surgery. Charlie looked at the pile of bandages and Cling Film wrap that he had wrapped him in to stop the blood from leaking over the seats in his Mercedes-Benz. "How are you, Glenn?"

"Not too bad accepts of this massive pain in my side." That's with Glenn you are stopping here at my house tonight you can have the spare room."

"No Charlie I will be all right here."

"Glenn you will do as you are told you is going to sleep in the spare room." I'm not leaving you lose in my wine cellar to drink all my wine."

LOL, "you are funny Charlie," Glenn said with a weak voice.

Charlie asks, "Do you feel comfortable enough to walk?" Glenn paused for a moment.

So Charlie replied, "I will get you the wheelchair." Charlie turned around and walked towards the back end of the wine cellar and pulled out a dusty old wheelchair, preceded to wheel it towards Glenn who by this time was coming around out of the anaesthetic quite well. And was starting to feel the pain in his side. Charlie opened up the wheelchair and helps Glenn onto it. Charlie then pushed him towards the door of the wine cellar as turned off the lights and pushed Glenn up the ramp into the garden and then walked back down to the wine cellar door and locked it shut. Walked back up towards Glenn and started pushing him into the house. Thankfully we have a spare room downstairs. "How do you feel Glenn?"

"Absolutely beautiful thank you very much, Charlie, you saved my life literally." Charlie carries on pushing the wheelchair through the little doorway into the ground floor bedroom. "Glenn what did you do with the keys?"

Glenn replies in a weak voice, "I left the keys in the ignition and the door unlocked hoping that somebody would steal the car. And the mobile phone was left on the passenger seat in plain view."

"Good job Glenn. But by the way, did you leave any blood stains in the car?"

"No bloodstains on the car the cellophane seem to have done the trick."

"Yes I know. I notice that there wasn't any leakages downside of the cellophane dressing."

"Come on Glenn let us get you into bed." With a little bit of a struggle, Charlie managed to help Glenn into his bed."

"I will be back in a few minutes Glenn."

Charlie walked out of the guest bedroom and back down into the cellar to clean up the bloody bandages and tidy his surgical tools away. Into the sterilising unit. Then he took the plastic bag up to the barbecue and also set these on fire with the bandages inside removing all evidence.

That Charlie went back into the cellar and collected a syringe filled with a painkilling drug and anticoagulant and a saline drip. He then took this up to Glenn and gives him the injections and administered the saline drip. Almost immediately after Charlie had given Glenn the injection he started to perk up quite considerably. "You can get some sleep now Glenn. I will be just outside the door."

"Okay, Charlie thanks you good night."

Charlie walked out of the door and turns the lights off and went to make himself-fresh coffee. At that moment to his amazement car lights flooded in through the window. Charlie looked over to the open door of the spare room so Charlie walked over to the spare room pulling the door closed slightly and having a quick look at Glenn lying there fast asleep. By the time, he turned around and walked back to his coffee. The lights had gone out in the car on the drive.

Charlie took a sip from his coffee just as his wife walked in. "hello dear." she says. "How was your day darling?" "I am so sorry I have been so late, but I do believe I have lost my phone." Helen carries on walking in and walked up to Charlie and gives him a big full hug. Charlie stands there like a cold fish while his wife is hugging him. Helen notices this straightaway.

"Have you had a very hard day-to-day darling you could say that?" Helen gives Charlie a friendly little kiss on his bottom lip.

"Dear, we have a guess this evening. He is asleep in the spare bedroom. As he is exhausted and he has also had a very busy day. And I'm also going to bed right now because I am shattered."

"Okay, a love I will be up shortly just after my drink." Helen blows a kiss. Charlie really didn't feel like replying to it.

And he just turned around and walked up the stairs into the bedroom. Charlie weighs up the calculations of his wife losing her mobile phone, as it may be as innocent as it may be. Charlie mulls over in his mind every scenario that you can think of. While he is getting dressed and ready for bed. By now Charlie is too tired to have any reliable thoughts, so I'm just going to have to sleep on it.

Charlie soon makes himself-comfortable in bed and curls up into a tight ball. He just thinks to himself-sold the promise. And soon Charlie is relaxed and drifting off to sleep.

Charlie did not fear his wife come into the bedroom that night. He only noticed that she was there in the early hours of the morning. It looks like we are going to have a lot to talk about. But 1st of all extract the information without her knowing that I am onto her.

CHAPTER 9

The dawn chorus of the tweeting birds singing breaks up the early-morning silence. Charlie slowly wakes up earlier than usual. He slowly opens his eyes to see his wife lying there comfortable with her eyes closed. He notices that she must have been in a rather big rush to get to bed last night. His wife missed half of her own eye with the make-up remover; it resembled a shadow of a shiny black eye. As Charlie's eyes came into focus. She is just so peaceful lying there with her eyes closed fast asleep. Charlie began to maul over this within his mind, "why would she not tell him that she had lost the phone. Well, we are just going to have to retrace the steps, Charlie fathoms on his first thoughts of questioning." Charlie peels back the bedclothes gently. And then slowly moves out of the bed. To leave his wife, they're sleeping. Walking towards the door grabbing his dressing gown off the back of the chair in a fluid movement while making his way towards the stairs. As quiet as a mouse, he walks down the stairs. And into the living room he notices that the spare bedroom door was closed, Charlie caringly takes this opportunity to have a look in on his friend Glenn. To see how he has managed with his injuries through the night.

Charlie quietly walks up to the door and rests his hand on the door handle for a moment, for a moment to hope and pray that everything will be all right. He slowly applies more pressure on the door handle and the door catch clicks, with a push on the door cautiously it swings open to reveal rumpled tangled bedclothes and a lot of congealed blood on the floor next to the bed. A plastic drain bottle lying on its side on the floor. The drainpipe that Charlie had inserted into Glenn surgical wound. Had pulled out of the bottle and spilt its contents on the floor. From the look of the bed covers it look like Glenn had a rather rough night. Charlie took a couple of steps forward into the room and moved towards the bed, Glenn was lying there on his back, and the intravenous saline I.V drip bag was nearly empty hanging from the headboard. Glenn looked so peaceful so Charlie moved in a little bit closer while holding his breath. Soon he noticed that the bedclothes were moving slightly as Glenn is breathing in and out. Charlie exhaled with relief and then turned around and walked out of the room after changing the I.V on the headboard. Charlie's concern for the patient was paramount, but breakfast was first on the agenda before he could manage to stomach cleaning up that blood or even waking up the patient. So Charlie then headed towards the kitchen to make breakfast and drinks for everyone first. Charlie knows that he has a difficult situation to face first thing in the morning and he would rather deal with the day on a full stomach. Charlie hunted around in the electric fridge for the eggs and a fresh loaf of bread. As he stood up from the refrigerator foraging he placed his hands on the counter and helped himself up into a standing position with his hands still on the worktop he bowed his head and tried to think things through for a moment. At least a minute had passed before he moved again. And then he reached for the large cooking pot with a nice sturdy wooden handle and solid steel base. Placing this on to the induction hob ring and he proceeded to crack the eggs into the glass, then he poured into the cooking pot the milk to bring to the boil, also blending in the eggs with the electric blender at the same time. Then Charlie laid out their cups out onto two trays plates salt-and-pepper also. Freshly ground coffee from the coffee percolator just began starting to percolate through the filter. The long shadows in the kitchen started to get shorter as the morning Sunrise takes effect. He gives the scrambled eggs a quick stir and then turns the grill on. Another minute on the induction hob bringing the mixture to the boil and he takes the hot pot off the induction hob and pushes it underneath the grill. And then concentrates on the toast. You can tell Charlie has got quite a bit on his mind this morning because the order of things that he did this morning were totally out of character. He pours the coffee. And at that moment he looks up to see a dark silhouette standing outside the front door. Charlie was startled from this heinous silhouette and grabs a large kitchen knife out of the butchers wooden block, he then started striding towards the door as he can hear the letterbox rattling; indeed a white envelope appears through the letterbox and drops onto the floor and the silhouette turns around and walks off down the path. Charlie carries on walking over towards the door with a knife in his hand. And bends over to pick up the envelope. Notices that it is addressed to himself. At that moment, his wife calls out. "What are you doing without the big knife," Charlie immediately makes a move and places the tip of the large kitchen knife behind the envelope flap and with one long stroke he cuts into the envelope flap to open it. "Just opening the mail dear."

Helen stopped dead in her tracks as an uncomfortable feeling came over her. As she had just felt like she had been threatened. But soon that passed and Helen began walking again towards the kitchen island and the coffee percolator. Charlie Laird at her, as Helen reaches towards the coffee percolator jug. Charlie is now slowly walking towards her with the big carving knife in his hand and a letter in the other side. Charlie was doing this purposefully to intimidate his wife. To see if she would crack under the strain. To notice if there was anything different within her personality that would come to light under a little piece of pressure. But now not a single flinch from Helen as she picked up the percolator coffee jug and started to pour it into the 3 cups. Charlie walked up behind her and plunged the large kitchen knife deeply and firmly back into the butchers Wooden Knife Block set. Helen says at that moment, "does Glenn take sugar in his coffee?" Charlie replies, "yes one sugar, but I will take it to him because there is a little mess on the floor."

"What is it?" she says. Charlie immediately replies, "is surgical drain has fallen out of the catch bottle and spilt on the floor."

Concerned, Helen says, "I hope it was not too much of a major operation for him. But what has happened?"

"I had to give him an emergency operation last night, I cannot tell you much more at the moment, but I will not be going to work today because I need to look after him."

"I totally understand darling, but I will also be stopping with you as it is my day off today. But that is terrible with Glenn, I will help you look after and I will clean it up you finish your breakfast off darling." The toast popped up, and Helen walked towards the little cleaning cupboard in the kitchen and grabbed her marigolds and other cleaning implements. And headed towards the ground floor bedroom. Charlie watched his wife walking with a bucket and mop in her hand and a semi-see-through dressing down as the early morning sunlight made it slightly transparent as she walked across the room, showing that figure. How could she just be so perfect Charlie thought to be self? As he was buttering toast. Cutting the slice from corner to corner and placing the two triangles on the plate either side one particular slice of toast. Charlie opened up the grill as his wife disappears into the spare bedroom. As she does her high-end private profile nursing?

He loads the dishwasher up and prepares the guests breakfast tray and carries it to the room. Charlie could hear Glenn was wide-awake as Glenn and my wife were both talking as Charlie entered the room with a breakfast tray, "good morning Glenn, how does the patient feel?"

Glenn replies, "as well as can be."

"There is your breakfast, that is good news." Charlie wields a mini table over towards Glenn. "It is certainly the finest private hospital that I have ever frequented."

Helen says, "you will soon change your minds Glenn when we send you the bill." the smile from Helen and a wink from Charlie. "No darlings do not make him laugh,"

"Right boys I will leave you to it, I hope you enjoy your breakfast that Charlie has cooked up Glenn."

"I am sure I will Helen on sure I will thank you very much for cleaning up after me."

"You are welcome my dear Charlie, you are definitely part of the family. Now you enjoyed if there is anything else that I can do please ask." Helen turns around picking up the mop and bucket and walks off into the kitchen.

"Anything said, Glenn?

"No questions asked no answers said.

You have a fine woman their Charlie."

"I know, just have to keep my head straight and not do anything silly to lose for or push her away. I just pray and hope that it is totally something innocent."

"I understand Charlie, it is something that cannot actually be talked about is that not it."

"Yes it will be quite traumatic for her if she ever found out."

Charlie says, "I am going to have to tell the truth sooner or later. So let us leave it at that I will think of something later. Now carry on with your breakfast. By the way how is the pain this morning?"

Glenn replies, while attempting to eat his scrambled egg on toast. "Further to moderate. Not too much pain only when I move, or breathe deeply."

"Do not do that too often. I will see you in a moment I have got to have my breakfast now."

Charlie turned on the television and gave Glenn the remote control. And soon walked out of the room.

Helen was sitting on the stall at the island having her breakfast, as Charlie approached Helen pointed her toe to the floor and then suggestively run her finger from below the knee all the way up her bare leg to her hip, attracting the gazing eyes of her husband.

"How is the breakfast, honey?"

"Delightful, you sexy man."

This took Charlie by quite a surprise as he reached the island and gazed into his wife's eyes.

"Thank you my love."

Then Charlie sat down next to her placed his hand upon her thigh and reached for the tray to pull towards himself with his breakfast on it. A slight dusting of pepper, a sip of coffee and the beautiful, gorgeous company of his wife over breakfast to the beginning of a new day.

Charlie thinks, I must rewind and think about the time when I was euphoric to ring my wife to tell the good news of my thoughts of our future.

Charlie says, "I have been thinking quite a lot about you in the last few days dear, and I have come to a conclusion about our future."

Helen pauses in mid-flow inputting a piece of scrambled egg on toast into her mouth on her fork. And waited in anticipation to receive the final few words from her husband.

Charlie says, "I am sure you will be happy with this, but first of all, I have to ask you. To make sure that you will be happy with this." As you can tell that Charlie was very nervous and he continues to say "I have put a great deal of thought into this. And I do believe that us as a couple, a happily married couple at that." By now Helen is sitting there with her mouth open slightly. You can see her mind thinking through her eyes but not coming up to the conclusion that Charlie was thinking or what she was thinking.

After taking a sip from his coffee, he continues to say, "I am happy to announce to you that I am willing and happy to have a baby with you as I know this will be a love child and I cannot just keep you all to myself or my life so I am willing to share you with our loving child all children, I am happy that I would like to start a family with you my darling."

Then Helen just popped the scrambled egg on toast into her mouth from the fork and then started chewing with the surprise of what her loving husband just said. This moment lasted a lifetime to Charlie waiting for the answer, but there was an expression of excitement that washed over his lovely wife. Her face lit up and then she turned her chair around to Charlie slowly. Swallowing her mouthful of scrambled eggs on toast. Jumped up off her chair in excitement and flung her arms around Charlie shoulders. Charlie stood still and they both embraced each other as Helen says, "yes I love you I love you I love you." Charlie replied, "I love you I love you I love you to my darling I love you I love you," the excitement of the romantic couple announcing their love between each other was heard from Afar, in other words, Glenn could hear them in the spare room. Even over the television.

Charlie then says, "Have you managed to get the booking for the vacation?" Helen replies, "Oh yes, my love and yes, we are travelling to the beautiful islands of "Greece Anastasis Apartments, Imerovigli, This hotel is like a dream... I love the views here if you recollect the last time we felt as if we were in paradise! Words can't describe the peace we felt while lying near the pool overlooking the water. The staff within the property the last time where there were just so absolutely incredible at making sure our stay last time was nothing less than PERFECT." As a second honeymoon would you just love this my love."

"Of course, darling, I said whatever holiday you wanted and this is the holiday you want so this is the holiday you are going to make the most romantic time of your life, with me." Helen replies, "of course it is with you darling, I would not want to depart on holiday with anybody else." Charlie answers, "Do we have the dates booked," "well, this is what I wanted to talk to you about so that we can arrange dates together." "Yes, we can do that today we can make the arrangements and get everything patched up today."

Helen is so very excited. Charlie could not believe that she would even think about having an affair. You know, Charlie loves his woman that much that if she received a one-off affair and kept it entirely secret from him and it did not interfere with their lives at all in any way, shape or form as much as he loved his wife, I am sure that Charlie would have turned a blind eye to protect the marriage of love as for some men it is quite different.

The illumination emanating from his wife's complexion smiles and excitement for the future made Charlie think why was he not doing this a year ago and go before.

I know which would be very cruel of me to turn round to you and say

The end

But in a manner of speaking it is the end of a single, married life but the beginning of a new journey.

To be continued.

With thanks to WH Smith Telford town centre

Lightning Source UK Ltd.
Milton Keynes UK
UKOW06f1641180116

266618UK00001B/21/P